"MAN THAT SHOT ME CAME TO FINISH THE JOB."

Trace stared around at what had been his front yard. Everything was destroyed; even the earth was trampled by cattle prints.

Dismounting, he walked quickly to the porch and found a wide open doorway, the door itself wrenched from its hinges. Inside was ruin. His furniture lay overturned, the wallpaper hanging in strips. In the kitchen, his stove was on its side, bedded in soot and broken dishes. Suddenly the still, hot peace was broken by the sound of a single rifle shot as Tracy dropped to the ground. . . .

Ernest Haycox

① SIGNET BRAND WESTERN

Exciting SIGNET Westerns by Ernest Haycox

(0451)

- ☐ **STARLIGHT RIDER** (123468—$2.25)*
- ☐ **BUGLES IN THE AFTERNOON** (114671—$2.25)*
- ☐ **CHAFEE OF ROARING HORSE** (114248—$1.95)*
- ☐ **RETURN OF A FIGHTER** (094190—$1.75)*
- ☐ **RIDERS WEST** (099796—$1.95)*
- ☐ **SUNDOWN JIM** (096762—$1.75)*
- ☐ **TRAIL SMOKE** (112822—$1.95)*
- ☐ **TRAIL TOWN** (097793—$1.95)*
- ☐ **CANYON PASSAGE** (117824—$2.25)*
- ☐ **DEEP WEST** (118839—$2.25)*
- ☐ **FREE GRASS** (118383—$2.25)*
- ☐ **HEAD OF THE MOUNTAIN** (120817—$2.50)*
- ☐ **SIGNET DOUBLE WESTERN: ACTION BY NIGHT and TROUBLE SHOOTER** (123891—$3.50)*
- ☐ **SIGNET DOUBLE WESTERN: SADDLE & RIDE and THE FEUDISTS** (094670—$1.95)
- ☐ **SIGNET DOUBLE WESTERN: ALDER GULCH and A RIDER OF THE HIGH MESA** (122844—$3.50)*

Prices slightly higher in Canada

Starlight Rider

By
Ernest Haycox

①
A SIGNET BOOK
NEW AMERICAN LIBRARY
TIMES MIRROR

PUBLISHER'S NOTE

This novel is a work of fiction. Names, characters, places, and incidents are either the product of the author's imagination or are used fictitiously, and any resemblance to actual persons, living or dead, events, or locales is entirely coincidental.

SIGNET TRADEMARK REG. U.S. PAT. OFF. AND FOREIGN COUNTRIES
REGISTERED TRADEMARK—MARCA REGISTRADA
HECHO EN CHICAGO, U.S.A.

SIGNET, SIGNET CLASSICS, MENTOR, PLUME, MERIDIAN AND NAL BOOKS are published by The New American Library, Inc., 1633 Broadway, New York, New York 10019

First Signet Printing, June, 1983

1 2 3 4 5 6 7 8 9

PRINTED IN THE UNITED STATES OF AMERICA

CHAPTER 1

---◆---

HUGH TRACY RETURNS

HUGH TRACY passed Indian Flat around seven of the morning, traveling fast and feeling only a slight pucker in his right flank where the bullet hole had been three months healing. High desert sunlight lay in stippled patches along the low pine-belted ridges, and the intervening gulch walls seemed a rawer red than he remembered them to be. Long absence had done this, had begotten a consuming hunger for home soil; thus when Dead Axle grade reached its summit and let him out upon a thousand-foot ledge, the scene rolling off yonder struck him straight between the eyes. Impatient as he was, he stopped to realize the picture that had been in his mind through so many weary days.

It was unchanged, changeless; and one cotton-white cloud fluff stood overhead in seemingly the same spot such a cloud had been the day of his ambush. The grand old scarps of Mogul and Powder rims—sheer and black faces confronting each other across nine miles of distance—took up a northern march, slimming into the far-off heat haze. Below and between ran the girted Powder desert, turned tawny by summer's ceaseless sun. Halfway up the valley and covered by Mogul's shadow, the buildings of Antelope town created indistinct outlines. Beyond that a lesser spur flanged out from Mogul, only a blue and blurred suggestion; but his eyes rested there longest.

"Well," he mused, "it is still there," and some nameless, clinging fear left him. He reached for his tobacco and curled a cigarette with fingers bleached a hospital white. Then, the smoke drawing well, he pressed down the trail somewhat recklessly. It was a full, fine feeling—to return erect and sound when he had never expected to return at all. Ninety days ago he had come up to this grade in the bottom of a flat-bed wagon, lying on a bloody mattress and deep in the fathomless pit whither a bullet had sent him. All he remembered of it now was insubstantial, like the misty phantasms of a bad dream—kerosene stench from a lantern, the jolt of the wagon, Bill Vivian's cursed-out rage.

5

Once his open eyes had recognized the polar star's timeless shining.

"But I'm back," he told himself, and felt the good heat loosening long-closed partitions in his body; this land was his medicine. At the bottom of the grade he swung into a road coursing diagonally across the Powder desert toward Antelope town in the distance. Alkali smell rose off the earth, and the miles of sage and mahogany bush and tumbleweed swept away. Dust devils swirled vagrant against the strengthening flare; the Vigilante tree stood alone as it always had. Nothing was changed.

Yet even as he said it his eyes—gray in humor, dull slate when angered—found change. The forward casting glance touched that point on the road where a plank bridge should have crossed Fetterman's dry creek bed, and found no bridge; nothing but charred fragments. Coming up, Hugh Tracy wheeled beside the depression and looked down. First inspection showed him something other than plain fire. In the rubbish was part of a double-tree, some bits of scorched harness, and the skeletal iron remnants of a wagon. He studied it with furrowed thoughtfulness until he had the story. And when he had the story, he dipped across the gully and went on. "Recent and plain enough," he muttered. "Harness means horses. Horses means somebody was pullin' a load across the bridge, and got stopped. Forcibly stopped."

That first scent of trouble perceptibly changed him. He pressed on, scanning the surrounding country with a sharper eye, sitting a little stiffer in the saddle, face more drawn together. He knew the Powder desert too well to be astonished, yet he had been away from it just long enough to let its antagonisms and flurries of violence soften in his mind. Now, less than a half-hour after entering the valley, he was bluntly reminded that he had to put up his guard again, and again travel with his senses whetted for the unexpected. His holiday was over, and he was back where he had been before the ambusher's bullet felled him.

At thought of it he grinned slightly, that slow shift of muscles pulling his naturally dark cheeks into a rather skeptical cast. The lines of his face were square and came to definite endings at chin, mouth, and neck. Black-haired, big-boned, he had a manner of tipping his head forward to study whatever stood in front of him with a long, slow inspection; and the deep gray of his eyes was apt to be expressive only when the combustible elements of his temper fused to produce a rough humor or an anger that flashed out hard and rebellious. The Powder desert knew him thoroughly and followed him with close interest. He never smoothed his words for policy, and his enemies, suffering from

6

the slashing roughshod manner of those words or from the effect of his big, ready fists, hated him thoroughly—as the bullet mark in his body testified. Yet Bill Vivian had cried openly at sight of Hugh Tracy lying half dead in the flat-bed wagon. He was twenty-five, physically powerful, always restless and unconforming; nor had anybody yet penetrated the widely varying and deeply accented tempers of this man to discover what made them so.

"You bet I'm back," he observed quietly, "and somebody will be interested to know that. Mighty interested."

Thus around high noon Antelope saw him come racking down the dusty street as of old. He sat straight in the saddle, both fists locked in front of him, elbows up; underneath a cream Stetson were features not quite as bronzed as the town remembered, but the gray eyes were as quick and direct and penetrating as ever.

For his part he was surprised at the quiet in Antelope on this, a Saturday afternoon. The hitch racks were mostly unoccupied, the walks deserted. One man slept in a chair beneath the stable arch, a pair idled at the hotel corner; and half a dozen sat on Lou Burkey's saloon porch. Reining beside the porch, he found himself wondering. He knew none of them, which was strange enough in a country where every rider could describe every other rider from memory; and as he stepped to the ground, he found himself carefully considered by all in that peculiar range manner which is level-eyed and without apology. Casually nodding, he spoke:

"Gentlemen, how."

A studied stillness held them. One man tipped his head, another poked back his Stetson with a thumb; and that was the sum of their answer. Hugh Tracy's mouth corners sagged a little, his stare hardened. If it wasn't hostility they displayed it was bad manners, and at no time was he disposed to ignore either condition. But there was an increase of puzzlement in him, and so he placed those six faces in a corner of his mind for future consideration and pushed through to the saloon's darkened interior. Here was more quiet emptiness. Lou Burkey stood alone behind his own bar and played solitaire, not looking up until he had shifted one card and tallied another on its ace.

Hugh Tracy grinned. "Good customer of yours has returned, Lou."

Lou Burkey's face was moon-round and olive, masked by a heavy mustache. At all times it was a good poker face, but Hugh, slowly ceasing to smile, saw some powerful thought shift the saloon-man into a heavy, self-conscious reserve. Burkey's lids slowly squeezed up into the light of enigmatic, copper-shaded eyes. Both pudgy palms turned downward on the bar. Nor could anything have been more lackluster than his greeting.

"Hello, Hugh."

"Hard to revive me, after tallyin' me for dead?"

Lou Burkey said: "You're twenty pounds short of what you was."

Tracy shrugged his shoulders. "I'll get that back. Push me over a drink."

"Where you goin' now?"

"Hell of a question! Home, of course. Where would you think?"

"Never do another man's thinkin' for him," said Burkey calmly.

"Do I have to write you a note about that drink?"

Burkey reached around, sent a glass spinning over the bar, placed a bottle carefully beside it. Tracy stared at the single glass, half offended. "What's the matter with you, man? Drink with me. It ain't every day a dead man returns to Antelope."

"No offense. My stomach is poorly." The saloonman turned to the cards and piled them together, beginning a haymow shuffle. The calculated indifference was too obvious to miss. Tracy downed his whiskey neat with an increase of irritation.

"What's happened to the usual Saturday gang around here?"

"Busy in the hills this year. Shiftin' cattle. It's been dry."

"Where's Bill Vivian?"

Burkey shook his head. "Ain't heard. Guess he got a sack of grub and took a long *pasear* for himself."

Hugh Tracy laid a quarter beside his glass, bringing Burkey's eyes right back to him. "Antelope," said he, deliberate enough, "is so dead it stinks and ought to be buried. And who are those tongue-tied gentlemen sunnin' their moccasins on your porch?"

"Shadrow's men."

Tracy's glance whipped back from the saloon windows and centered on Lou Burkey's moon cheeks. "Look here, is he importing hands——"

"I'm all out of answers," said Lou Burkey. "Hughey, no hard feelin's, if you please. But I'm not your friend. Not these days."

Tracy grunted, suddenly catching on. The rebuff left him without anger. This was Powder desert, and this was what he returned to; schemings and contrivings, threats and some form of vengeance by day or night—all this heavy current of intrigue beneath the apparent calm of the land. He ceased to be puzzled. For, without knowing what this game might be, he realized it

8

was a part of an older game never played out. A small contempt of Lou Burkey, of whom he once had thought better, took hold of him. Bone and blood an individualist, there was nothing in life Hugh Tracy hated more than pressure. He fought it savagely, instinctively, without bothering to furnish a reason for his fighting. Another man's buckling under roused only his scorn. His words went flat.

"I told you something was dead around here."

"Careful," said Burkey, so rapidly that Tracy straightened, half thinking the saloonman meant to make a quarrel of it. But he was mistaken. Burkey's head twitched slightly toward the porch. Out there the murmur of talk had ceased. Tracy grinned and walked casually from the place. The six were postured as they had been before, excepting one man who stood now near the door. Gathering up his reins, Tracy made a general observation at them.

"If you boys work for Tade, don't let him find you wearin' the seat off your britches. Tade's peculiar in that respect."

The man nearest the saloon door struck instantly back. "Who in hell was talkin' to you?"

"And you're not dumb, like I thought!" marveled Tracy, ironically. The grin returned, hard and sharp. "Now that you mention it, nobody's talkin' to me. But I'm talkin' to you. Objections?"

The man stared, flashed a sudden side glance at his partners, and pulled his thin lips together. When he spoke again it was with considerable less hostility. "Go sleep it off."

"The crushing answer of a bright mind," applauded Tracy.

"Look here," snapped the other. "Who stepped on your corn?"

"I was taught as a little boy," said Tracy, "that it was just politeness to answer a man's greetin'. Hate to have a howdy bounce back in my face."

The other stood fast, more and more watchful, apparently warned by Tracy's ready sarcasm. Tracy gathered the reins. "Better go tell Tade I'm back—that Hugh Tracy is back. He'll love to hear it." And he walked the pony over to the stable trough. The fellow under the arch still slumbered, or seemed to, and after a short survey, Tracy cantered on down the street. He passed a row of poplars, skirted the picket fence of Antelope's graveyard. Looking in, he caught the mark of change once more in the form of a fresh mound of broken dirt; instantly apprehensive—for he was thinking now of Bill Vivian—he rode in and looked down at the new headboard.

It read: "*Charley Sullivan. ?—1893.*"

The hocks of Hugh Tracy's horse had no more than beat up Antelope's dust when Lou Burkey came out of his saloon and interrupted the talk passing between the six hands.

"Get this right," said he. "You follow Tracy's advice. Go tell Tade Shadrow he came back—that Tracy came back."

The one who had absorbed Hugh Tracy's sarcasm showed the rankling resentment in him by snapping up the saloonman's words. "Get what right? Who the hell is Tracy?"

"Was you longer in this country," said Burkey, "you'd know without a doubt. I'm telling you. Tade never put you boys here to pick daisies. Let him know about Tracy or he'll take a hack outa your hide."

"Tracy," said the other man, repeating the name slowly. "Seems like I heard of him over in the Dog Rib country."

"He's made enough noise in Powder durin' his time to be heard of farther off than that," answered Burkey. "Ain't anybody on the ranch give you the McCoy about Hugh Tracy?"

"No," said the man. "Nobody has. We only went to work for Shadrow a week ago. And he camped us here. All we know is to stand around and wait for orders."

"Well," grunted Burkey, "you didn't hire to punch cows, did you?"

The man gave him a quick, alert glance. "What we hired for is entirely our business."

"You're not foolin' anybody. Antelope knows more about this than you do. We grew up in this grief. You only been lugged into it as paid guns. Don't essay any mystery."

"I was askin' about Tracy," grumbled the man. "What's he got to do with it?"

"Right at this minute he's got everything to do with it," said Burkey and looked down the road at Tracy's subsiding dust. "That fellow's been gone from here the last three months. He's been outside, in a hospital. He got a bullet right in his side one day on account of ridin' too close to the rim."

"Dry-gulched?"

"Well," said Burkey ironically, "you do your guessin'. Anyhow, he never knew who picked him off. Anybody but Tracy it'd killed. So he's back, lookin' for the gun that matches the slug that hit him —and the fellow behind it. Like I say, you better go tell Shadrow he's here."

"Oh," grunted the man, lifting his eyebrows. "That's it, uh? What's he got Shadrow wants?"

Burkey's answer was swift enough. "Who said anything about that? You blamed fool, keep your thoughts inside that coco of yours."

"Yeah?" said the man, and added a grinning, "well, we're glad to know the two is old-time friends. Still, what's this lad Tracy got which anybody else might want?"

"He lives," said Burkey idly, "on a spur off Mogul down yonder. I've heard it told the only piece of water in ten miles is in Tracy's front yard."

"And how long's this been goin' on?"

Burkey turned into his saloon. "Well, Tracy was shot three months ago, wasn't he?"

The Shadrow hand swung on his partners. "Now maybe this Tracy sport don't know who hit him, but he sure had all the earmarks of a fella pointed the right way. I guess I better ride along to the ranch."

One of the others said: "The hell of walkin' cold into a country, like us, is we don't never know what the rest of the misery may be. I always heard Powder was damned full of peculiar angles. I'd say there's more to this than so far published."

"You're paid well, ain't you?" asked the first hand, and went off to his horse.

Tracy came out of the graveyard and followed the desert road northward, overshadowed by Mogul's rearing face. Heat fog deepened out on the flat, and refracting layers of hot air trembled up from the baking earth. A small bunch of cattle lay widely scattered.

"So it's good-bye Charley," he muttered. "A fine fellow and too healthy to die of natural causes. It was a horse that piled him or a man that piled him. And it is mighty odd he should be buried over on the Testervis side of the grave lot. He never'd been a Testervis hand up till three months ago. What's happened in this damned scope of country?"

He had come forty miles since daylight and was a little weary. The gunshot scar now and then knotted the muscles of his flank, and he found it harder to swing with the horse. Irritated by this feeling of physical inefficiency, he remembered the time he had racked sixty miles to Red Bridge School, danced all night, and had ridden the same distance home. Yet as the road passed under his feet he kept the pony to a steady lope, drawn on by the sight of that foothill flanging out from Mogul ahead. At Twenty Mile Rock he stopped to water at a small spring encased in a bottomless galvanized tub; an hour afterwards he flanked the TS—Tade Shadrow's brand—rim road climbing a fault in Mogul's face.

"Better than odd," he reflected, still thinking of Charley Sullivan, "to find him among the Testervis dead ones. Never knew it to fail—one death in this country is sign of another. Got to find Bill Vivian and get the news."

Mogul's parapet and that of Powder across the desert began to descend gently and spread farther apart, creating a vast bay to the yonder north. Off there the haze was gradually penetrated by the outline of rolling hills; and directly ahead the spur toward which he had been urging the horse all this day flung out its foot slopes to meet him. He passed up the incline eagerly, identifying every depression and mark. A considerable stand of pine studded the spine of the spur. Narrow fingers of verdant growth ran down against the sere, puma-colored bunch grass and hardpan—unvarying sign of water in a dry land. Three hundred feet off the desert floor, and some twelve miles from Antelope, he entered the shade and followed a beaten trail, more eager than he thought he ever could be. Around the bend and within a rimming edge stood a meadow whose surface was occupied by a frame house, a small barn, and lesser outbuildings.

"Home is home, in anybody's language." Then a short circle of the path brought him full upon the yard—and all his senses of pleasure died.

Around him was the mark of malicious intrusion. Of the fence which he had so painstakingly put up one winter's month there was now no sign except an occasional pole. The wire had been stripped off, carried away, and the wood piled and burnt. He saw the charred areas where the fire had been made. Prints of cattle hoofs stood throughout the yard, and as he went forward to the watering trough he found the surrounding ground churned to loose mud. Something had happened in the barn, too, but his immediate thought was for the house. Dismounting, he walked to the porch and faced a wide open doorway, the door itself wrenched from its hinges and standing awry against the wall. Inside, where all things had been kept with a bachelor's neatness, was ruin. His furniture lay overturned, the wall paper hung down in slashed strips, marauding stock had broken his floor boards. The spoor of cattle was all through the place. Not a single glass pane remained undestroyed, his bunk frame was torn out of the wall. In the kitchen he found his stove on its side, bedded in soot and broken dishes. All the cupboard doors were open and the shelves bare.

He stood in the midst of this wreckage, filled with violent fury, big fists clenched and swinging helpless at his sides. And it was a long interval before he stirred from his tracks, to reach down and rescue the only thing in the place that had apparently escaped destruction—a single white cup. Unconsciously methodical, he righted a capsized table, laid the cup on it, and walked slowly back to the porch. Halted there, the lassitude of weariness and discouragement creeping like a disease through him in spite of his actual rage, he made his conclusions.

"Man that shot me came to finish the job."

He crossed to the west end of the proch and stared toward the higher elevation of land where the spur made jointure with Mogul's plateau. In that direction the glare of the down-plunging sun rose like the red guttering of a mountain fire, and broad bands of gold swept overhead. Thinking to himself, "In the morning I'll trace these cattle tracks," he turned back to unsaddle his horse; and it was then, hard on the heels of the thought, that the still, hot peace of the ridge was broken by the spanging echo of a rifle shot. The bullet went through the house wall a good ten feet from him with a quick and small and crushing sound.

His reaction was immediate. He dropped to the porch, rolled rapidly, and fell off the edge. From that protecting angle he raised his head and swept the pines and the lifted ground beyond the rim of Mogul, over where the repercussions of the shot still rolled out. Closely watching, he caught the quick flash of a metal bit hidden somewhere in the rock litter, perhaps six hundred yards removed.

"Won't have to wait for morning," grunted Tracy. Rising, he made a run for his horse.

CHAPTER 2

LYNN ISHERWOOD

BETWEEN porch and horse was a space of forty yards within the marksman's direct range. Charging across the yard, he expected a following shot to reach out after him; but none came, and he threw himself into the saddle with a small sense of relief. He aimed at the trees, reached this safety, and spurred up a trail. Day's brightness slowly subsided, and the first purple tints of twilight were filtering between the pines, deceptively shading the thin underbrush and each hoisting fold of the slope. He was badly stung; and when so, always reckless. Thus he went full tilt up the trail, relying on his first judgment as to the other man's whereabouts, not stopping until the pines petered out into an extraordinary rocky area encircled by a wall rising sharply some thirty feet—the topographical limit of Mogul proper.

At this point he reined behind a buckbrush clump and studied the parapet closely. The rail he now occupied reached that high ground via a fissure, but he rejected the approach, knowing the marksman was somewhere within shouting distance of the spot. The only other way of getting on top of the rim was by a fan-shaped causeway of rubble about a hundred yards ahead. Swinging his horse, he raced for it.

It exposed him again. Riding well over in the saddle, he watched the parapet jealously, and when he hit the foot of the causeway it was with spurs biting in, to reach the rim's top at a rush. Nothing stood in front of him. Mogul's sweep of plateau was bare as far as he could see; yet the next moment he fell from the saddle and started off on the run, revolver lifted. The ambushing party, he thought savagely, was waiting for another try, and should be accommodated. Throwing himself into a gully, he followed it quite a distance and rose behind a rock cone. Powder desert lay far below, and his own house was in sight. Halted, he thought he heard the stir of a body beyond the cone.

His answer was to reach for a small rock, throw it to the right of the cone and himself lunge around the left side, revolver risen again. What he saw so shocked him that the weapon sagged in

14

his fist. A woman stood there—a woman not long out of girlhood. She had a rifle in her arms, a rifle swinging around to cover him. Behind the lined sights were the most alive and interesting gray-blue eyes Hugh Tracy had ever seen—crowded now by an enormous anger. She said nothing at all, but he knew purpose when he met it, and he guessed that the small white finger resting on the trigger had squeezed out most of the slack. Motionless, he drawled a quiet phrase:

"If you can't find horns on the beast, it ain't legal to shoot him."

Her reply was a quick shift of her head. She lifted her eyes from the sights, caught his face. Next moment the rifle fell away. A queer rush of breath came from her throat, a faint and startled, "Oh!" A widening glance swept him head and foot. "Were you down at that house when—when I fired?" she demanded.

"Exactly. Now, do you locate any antlers on me?"

She shook her head with the air of not hearing him. Color went from her clear cheeks and came back again to stain them more deeply. Her eyes, remarkably direct and honest, met his return inspection.

"Would you believe me," she asked swiftly, "if I said I had no intention of hitting you?"

"I have been shot at before," said Hugh cheerfully, "but not by women, as a rule. Certainly I believe you. What's this all about?"

"No," she broke in, holding steadily to her point. "You don't understand yet what I mean. Supposing you were the man I thought was down there. Would you believe I hadn't shot to kill you—but only to warn?"

"The bullet hit ten feet to one side," said Tracy. "Are you a good enough shot to miss deliberately?"

"The bullet struck where I wanted it to," retorted the girl.

"But I wasn't the right man?"

"No."

Tracy said: "That's different."

"What are you thinking?"

"That the rest of this affair is entirely none of my business."

Her lips tightened, and he saw a quicker breathing disturb her breasts. "You are wrong," she said, throwing the contradiction at him.

"About it being none of my business?"

"No. About the reason why you thought it was none of your business."

That frankness astonished him. The grave, weighing glance clung to him without confusion; and in the interval Hugh Tracy was warmed by an agreeable discovery. This girl was close to being a beauty. He had at first, misled by the rough commonness of the man's clothing she wore, thought her unprepossessing. With the leisure to observe, he was aware of a fine and rounded modeling of body, a lithe strength apparent in her carriage. She was straight and slim and poised. A shaggy man's shirt, open at the throat, showed the graceful swell of shoulder and breasts. The coloring of her eyes, acccented by the low-slung brim of her hat, created one long shadow across a face slightly triangular. All the feminine softness was there, but made oddly striking by small, high cheekbones, and by the further symmetrical contour of neck and temple. Edges of ash-blonde hair showed beneath the hat. So much for physical outlines; yet beyond these swiftly registered impressions was a far stronger one of alertness and vitality.

She disturbed him with another short, direct question:

"Well, what are you going to do next?"

"Nothing," said Hugh, "except go home and forget it."

She shook her head, faint humor in her lip corners. "You won't. You'll never quit wondering. Well, you've got something coming to you by way of amend. Go ahead—ask it."

"No. I still insist it is your business. But look here. I have lived around the Powder a considerable number of years without noticing anybody of your description. Who are you?"

"Lynn Isherwood. Do you know any more about me now?"

He thought about it, shook his head. "Closest Isherwoods I know live away over in Malheur country."

"No relation. My branch lived in Nevada."

"Visiting here?"

"Staying here," said the girl, with a sort of breathless emphasis.

"Where?"

She didn't answer immediately, but slowly pivoted on her heels and looked down at his ranch lying beneath the gathered twilight. Powder desert shifted to a blue, limitless gulf, and Powder rim across the flat stood in this brief hour with every gigantic embattlement dripping cobalt color. First evening's cool came gently out of the west; the jagged edges of the broken ground around them slowly took on the shape of night. The girl swung back, definite features marred by a faint erasure of wistfulness.

"I think I had better not tell you where I live."

He lifted his palms in a gesture of resignation, and the girl spoke again.

"That's the second time you haven't pressed the point. Thank you."

"In this case," drawled Hugh, "I will not suppress the curiosity as a gentleman should. If you are staying in the Powder, my secret agents will find out where."

"Better if you didn't," she warned him. "Isn't it my turn now? Who are you?"

"To wit: Hugh Tracy, owner of that yonder piece of land on which you plunked a shot."

"Why—!" exclaimed the girl, jerking up her chin. It was half dark now, and he thought that was her reason for stepping a pace closer. But the light of her glance was so quick and alive that he guessed another reason. He drawled:

"I'm the wolf with the long teeth that folks tell the little girl about, to be certain she stays in bed."

"I have heard about you," admitted Lynn Isherwood.

"But not from folks who would know much good of me."

"I have heard about you from almost every man or woman I know or have met since I came here," said she. After a short pause, she went on: "Disregarding the weather, I guess you are the staple of conversation in this country."

Hugh Tracy's chuckle was dry, ironic. "I just aggravate some people."

"Yes? I think I know why—now."

"Go ahead."

"No. But do you know how I had you pictured, hearing all these things said?"

"Sure. I'm a fellow with a granite face—a black, beetling mug. When I laugh, it's like a file goin' the wrong way across a saw. I possess neither charity, faith, nor hope, and I have wrecked more barrooms than Carrie Nation, for different cause. The things I do make no sense to the citizens, and they have ceased to figure why any more. I fight for the pleasure of it. I'm too restless to stay on a job any given length of time. If there is ever any trouble around Powder, the first thing folks want to know is, where was Hugh Tracy? That's the picture you had."

"Why—yes," said Lynn Isherwood, showing surprise. "How could you know?"

"I know."

"That is half of the picture. What is the other half?"

"Isn't any."

She watched him for a long while, and he saw her lips purse.

17

A piece of a smile came to her face. "Just as well, then, that you think so."

"It's dark," said Hugh. "You'd better get on the road to home."

She turned away and climbed out of the depression, disappearing in another. When she reappeared she was asaddle, and she halted some fifty feet from him with a small, gay laugh falling across the dark. "If I came nearer, you'd read this pony's brand and know where I belonged."

"I will know soon enough."

"Hugh Tracy—don't find me. Please don't."

This time he refused to let the statement ride. "Is there any good reason why I shouldn't?"

"Trouble."

"Who for?"

"You," said she, reluctantly.

"Good-night," said Hugh. "And if you are crossin' this Mogul plateau, don't leave the beaten road at any time. You'd get lost in a minute. Not only that but—"

"Yes?"

"You've heard enough wolf stories," said he.

"All right," answered Lynn Isherwood. "I know what you mean. Remember, I have lived in this sort of country all my life—in Nevada. Thanks again, for not asking me what you wanted to ask. And, by the way, there is another side of the Hugh Tracy controversy. I have heard all of it, and I know. Good-night."

He watched her until she vanished behind the screen of darkness. Long after, when the last clacking echo of her pony dimmed in the south, he went to his own horse and rode homeward. Making a quiet survey of the yard, he spread his blankets in the wrecked house. He had not eaten since breakfast, and his bones ached with that weariness which fights off sleep. Lying face upward to the black ceiling, he realized he would never be able to light a lamp inside his house until Powder country had changed its appointed ways—and until he had met a man.

CHAPTER 3

·····•···◆···•·····

REACH OF THE OCTOPUS

ON MOGUL'S vast plateau, eleven miles southwest of Hugh
Tracy's place as the road runs, lay Tade Shadrow's home ranch—
nerve center of eighty thousand owned acres and of twice as
much government free range. That most of the TS had been
fraudulently acquired was common knowledge; that the threat of
Shadrow's power kept others from grazing their cattle on the free
range within his orbit of influence was always crystal clear. This
sort of ruthless and efficient acquisition was too generally accepted in the West to be considered a sin, except by the injured
parties. These, Shadrow had ample means of hushing. It was a
land of big outfits—being too dry for the small nester—and all of
them played the same jealous, watchful game, asking only that
the law let them alone in their fighting.

TS home quarters was a depressing place, without a tree to
shade it and without a single grace to redeem the squat ugliness
of its sunbeaten, paintless, frowsy buildings. During the beginning and end of seasons enough men passed through it to vote
the county any given way, as Shadrow very shrewdly understood,
but otherwise TS riders roamed far out and headquarters huddled
somnolent and dreary under the sun. One dusty road led along a
tangle of corrals and barns to a plaza, around which stood the
sheds, the shops, the store, the bunkhouses, the mess hall.
Exactly at such an angle in this plaza as to command every point
of activity sat the main house—a long, low structure galleried on
three sides. Tade Shadrow's office ran the length of the house of
the front side, and here he sat at present, doing what he had
often done before and doing it very well—firing a hand.

The hand stood in the middle of the room, hat crushed in one
hand; a lank young man with agate-green eyes and a raw red face
flushed to deeper crimson by a stubborn anger not altogether
unmixed with worry. Shadrow was in a chair behind his desk,
badly aged at sixty. Worth a fortune, he showed the unkempt
condition of a twenty-dollar hand. His suit was shabby, wrinkled;
his white shirt looked to have been slept in. He was smallish and

scrawny, and his head, the only well-developed part of him, hung forward on a thin neck. Beneath an utterly hairless crown was a face infinitely lined—shrewd with an animal shrewdness. A straggling sorrel mustache guarded thin lips made thinner by pressure; a nose, narrow and long, swooped out from between close-placed eyes. In those eyes was the only visible sign of remaining vigor. Dark and half-lidded, they burned with an intense energy. And it was evident that, as much as the hand disliked the scene, old Tade Shadrow enjoyed it.

"When I hire a man," said he in a grumbling, singsong voice, "I hire him to do like I say."

"I rode that line," said the hand doggedly. "I was there all the time."

"Look here, Bones, don't contradict *me!* You was seen two nights ago way to hell and gone over in Testervis country. Ain't that right, Tolbert? Wasn't he seen?"

Bones shifted and looked around at the third man in the room, who was the TS foreman. Inordinately tall and shackle-jointed, Tolbert's face was hard and smooth and expressionless. All he did now was slightly nod.

"You bet he was," said Tade Shadrow.

"Never denied it, did I?" retorted Bones. "I was chasin' strays like I told you."

"Ha—strays thirteen miles north of you!" ridiculed Shadrow. "It won't work."

Bones flared up. "You and your damned job can go take a runnin' leap in the ocean. Pay me off and I'm glad to shake the dust of this penny-pinchin', haywire, louse-bound outfit from my feet! I wouldn't work no more for an old scoundrel like you if I starved!"

Shadrow looked over to his foreman, slyly amused. "Hard, ain't he? Well, Bones, I've seen harder mugs and I've fired 'em, too. You know what I think? I think you're too crooked for me, that's what. Any hand that takes TS money and goes driftin' towards the Testervis boys will bear watchin'. It's lucky for you I don't ride you out of my yard on a pole."

"Give me my pay," muttered Bones.

"You'll get it," grumbled Shadrow, and reached for his work ledger. When he turned the pages, his face assumed a pinched expression. "You been here," he said reluctantly, "six months."

"Seven," contradicted Bones, wary-eyed.

"Dammit!" shouted Shadrow, slamming the flat of his hand on the table. "I said six! Here it is in the books! Stand there and try to beat me out of a month's pay, will you?"

Bones stirred, looked again at the foreman so quiet and still behind him. "All right," he said, wearily, "Let it ride as six."

"Store bill," mused Shadrow, following his tracing finger, "is a hundred and eight dollars and ninety-seven cents."

Bones walked forward, holding out his hand. "Something wrong there. Let me see that book."

Shadrow closed the ledger and put his hand across it, erupting again. "Bones, by the forked tail of old Billy, I'll stand no more from you! It looks to me like you're huntin' trouble, and I'm tellin' you this is a mighty good place to get it!"

Bones halted. "That store of yours is so rotten it stinks. Three prices for everything and none of it fit to carry off. I never bought that much, I'm tellin' you."

"And thirty dollars you borrowed a couple months ago," said Shadrow rapidly, "which leaves forty-one, naught three." He reached for a slip of paper and held it toward Bones. "There's your check for forty-one dollars even. The three cents ain't of any account to you."

Bones seized the check, stared at it. He put it in his pocket, big fist having trouble getting out again. Without a word—Tolbert and Shadrow watching him closely—he went to the door. In the opening he swung swiftly about.

"Shadrow, you never did an honest lick in your life," he yelled, bitterly outraged. "And you've done cheated me by a good eighty dollars! You miserable skinflint, that'll come floatin' home to you one day! Mark my word!" He threw himself backward, and a little later the two men heard him drum out of the yard.

Shadrow emitted a dry, pleased chuckle and settled in the chair. "Hey Tolbert? Ain't that the way to do it? They holler, but it don't help 'em none. Saved the price of two good steers on that fellow."

Lake Tolbert moved away from the wall and sat down, long legs folding up in front of him. He shifted his chew to let out a taciturn phrase. "He'll go to the Testervis side."

"No, he won't," contradicted Shadrow. "The Testervis boys wouldn't hire a man who had worked for me."

The foreman only said: "He'll essay to get his eighty dollars somehow."

"Of course he will," agreed Shadrow. "That's why I sent for Sid Maunders. Ain't he here yet?"

Tolbert shook his head, whereat Shadrow drummed his knuckles impatiently on the desk top and fell to grumbling. "There's another gentleman getting mighty fancy. He takes his own good

21

time comin' on my call. Independent as a hog on ice. One of these bright days I'll have to knock his ears back and run him off.''

"You won't," was the foreman's impassive answer.

"No?" growled Shadrow, irritable again. He stared at Tolbert, sly and knowing glance sliding over the other's blank cheeks. "Why won't I?"

Tolbert said nothing, and Shadrow's lip corners went downward. "I know men. He'd cut my throat if he could. For that matter there ain't a hand on this ranch who wouldn't steal from me. Not a one, Tolbert.''

"Leave me out of that," murmured Tolbert.

Shadrow's glance sharpened. "I wonder. I'd give a lot to know what's goin' on inside that head of yours. Nobody can read your face.''

"Do what you want, don't I? Fetch and carry. Back you up. Keep my mouth shut about what I know.''

The cataloguing of these virtues seemed to bother Shadrow. "Never mind," he grunted. "I ain't quarrelin' with you.''

The clatter of a pony's hoofs beat across the hard-packed yard, and a deep, surly voice said: "Stop fiddlin' or I'll saw your confounded jaws apart. I don't like this starvation stop no more'n you do.'' Lake Tolbert's steady stare met Shadrow's eyes and appeared to indicate something. The light coming through the doorway was blocked off by a body almost square from shoulder to hip. Two heavy, hair-felted wrists clung to a blackened belt. A columnar neck rose straight to small, flat ears, and beneath the the flare of a low-crowned hat was a broad face studded by two dull and insolent eyes.

"Broke both legs gettin' here," grumbled Shadrow, sarcasm edging the words.

"If I don't suit, hire another man," retorted Maunders, as acid as his chief.

Shadrow's big head shot forward. Across the usually petulant countenance sprang a cold, feral expression. It changed him so much that both other men turned alert. "This," said Shadrow, "may be a desolation stop to you, Mister Maunders, and your good time may be too important to waste on a ranch which pays you wages nowise in keeping with your undoubted worth. Nevertheless, when I call you, come. There is no wall-eyed, jug-headed son of a biscuit around here as can teach me to suck eggs. That applies to you, Mister Maunders.''

The tongue-lashing took Maunders aback. He threw an astonished side glance at the foreman, then said, less boldly: "Well, I'm here, ain't I?"

Shadrow moved around in his chair, fell to rapping out a rhythm on the desk with his fingers. "But not for long. I fired Willy Bones a minute ago."

Maunders looked a question.

"He considers himself grieved," Shadrow went on, "and like all other damn fools he'll essay to steal beef off me. There's too much of that among the riders of this ranch, and it is high time they had an example set."

Silence came, broken only by Shadrow's drumming on the desk. All the hatchet sharpness of his face appeared in strong relief, and his eyes burned brilliantly. Maunders stood still, not shifting his attention. Tolbert tipped his head to the ceiling.

"Bones will go right for the piece of country he knows best—back of Antelope, where Mogul feeds off towards Two Spot Butte. Ride now so you can get planted when he gets there. If he don't do anything, follow him till he does."

Lake Tolbert brought his head down to Shadrow, small hard lines springing around the noncommittal eyes; and as the three confronted one another, Willy Bones's fate was sealed beyond a doubt. Once more it was Shadrow who broke the spell, lifting an impatient hand. "Get goin', Sid."

"Write me out a requisition on the store for grub."

Instantly Shadrow turned querulous. "Can't you turn around without wantin' somethin'? You left here last time with ten days' provisions and you was only gone a week. Where's the other three days' stuff?"

"Gave it to a Testervis hand I found hungry," said Maunders, ironically. "Listen, Shadrow, I don't see why in thunder you got me and Tolbert on your payroll at all, considerin' how you pick at us."

It seemed to strike Shadrow as being funny, for he grinned and let out a squeaky "he-he." He looked at the big gunman. "Don't you know? Tolbert's to keep you honest and you're to see Tolbert don't doublecross me." Still chuckling, he reached for his pencil and a slip of paper. The other two swapped quick glances, and then Maunders said, "Add a couple boxes of shells to that requisition."

"Another dollar fifty," muttered Shadrow, bowed over his pencil. "What in nation do you do with all that lead?"

"Use it on company business."

Shadrow reared back. "That reminds me. Hugh Tracy come home yesterday."

The effect on Maunders was to drag him out of his imbedded stolidity. Brighter light quickened the dull eyes, the flat-featured face lengthened in astonishment. He hauled himself erect, shot a swift question at Shadrow.

"Where is he now?"

"Don't know. At his ranch, maybe."

"And you send me sashayin' off after Willy Bones when this Tracy is around?" demanded Maunders. "What's the matter with your head?"

"If you had my head," snapped Shadrow, "you'd be rich."

"Well," insisted Maunders, "what are you goin' to do about it? Leave him run loose?"

"That's best, for now."

"Not in my mind," countered Maunders. "I'm the fellow who—"

"Who takes orders," finished Shadrow. "Here's your requisition. And on second thought maybe you had ought to practice hittin' somethin' for a change. Tolbert, where you goin'?"

The foreman had risen and turned to the door. "Ain't you finished?"

"No," said Shadrow. "I've got something serious to say to the both of you. We've been snoozin' long enough. I ain't had a word for three days as to what the Testervis boys are doin'. Can't seem to find out. If it was only Bat in charge I wouldn't worry a minute, for he ain't got brains to do anything but fight. But Morgan's so condemned pious he might think of any sort of trick. I don't propose to be caught with my suspenders droopin', you hear me? So listen. We shift a crew of men northward. Take care of it, Tolbert. About thirty men. Do it tonight, after dark. See that the outfit floats pretty close to the Testervis line—back of Tracy's five or six miles. And stay there. You may not know it, but this business is about ready for boilin'."

Tolbert said, "All right," without inflection and swung into the doorway again. But Maunders stood fast, shaking his head. "I don't see—" he began, and was stopped by the foreman who, swinging sharply back from the porch, motioned rapidly with one arm.

"Speakin' of Tracy, he's comin' down the road."

Maunders wheeled completely around, ripped out an oath. Shadrow rose from his chair and for the first time showed concern. "Who's with him?"

"Nobody."

"Here," said Shadrow, snapping his fingers anxiously at the

24

foreman, "you stand where you was when Bones come in. Maunders, go to that far corner—"

"Not now," contradicted Maunders. "I don't want to meet him in here. Too close quarters. I'll go out back and wait in the yard."

"He's a damned fool for comin' to TS alone," grunted Shadrow. "Tolbert, if you see him make any move, stop it."

The tall foreman stood against the wall, coldly quiet, looking at the two others with the faintest expression of contempt visible in the veiled eyes. Shadrow sat down again and took to twisting his pencil between his fingers; Maunders, sullen hostility written over his flat face, slowly backed to an inner door and opened it. All of them heard Tracy drum across the yard and dismount on the porch.

"I'll do all the talkin'," said Shadrow in a sibilant undertone.

"Do that," drawled Tolbert, so queerly that Shadrow's glance whipped back to the foreman and clung there a long moment. But he had no chance to speak, for as Sid Maunders retreated through the inner door and softly closed it, Hugh Tracy entered from the porch.

Halted there, Hugh instantly understood that he walked into an arranged scene. The click of the inner door warned him, Lake Tolbert was rigid against the wall, and Shadrow's position behind the table showed strain. The eyes of the TS owner, full of sly calculation, gave the lie to his friendly greeting.

"Hugh, it's like old times to see you here. Sit down."

"I'll stand," was Hugh's dry answer, and he walked across the room and turned to better command these two men posted on his flanks. He inclined his head at Tolbert, realizing clearly the purpose of the foreman's presence. A floor board in an adjoining room squealed under pressure; Shadrow broke into sudden talk.

"So the old hell-raisin' Hugh is among us again! I'll say, though, that you appear a little peaked to me."

"Such personal interest moves me deeply," drawled Hugh.

"Oh go on! Can't you never take a man's word for what it's worth? You make a heap of enemies thataway, Hugh. Too confounded skeptical. Always lookin' at the teeth of the horse."

"And so do you."

Shadrow grinned his wry, knowing grin. "Havin' money, everybody tries to make a sucker outa me. But I guess I've sold as many bum critters as I've bought."

Tracy nodded, reaching for his cigarette articles. The black head went thoughtfully downward during the manufacturing of the smoke, and the broad, blunt fighter's features remained inscrutably grave. Shadrow, never liking these deadlocked silences, fiddled a little and winked at Tolbert.

"Well, Hugh, what's on your mind?"

Tracy held the completed smoke in one hand and stared at Shadrow. "Tade, what do you know about the wreckin' of my place?"

"Not a thing," said Shadrow, promptly. "Not a blessed thing. Some of the boys passed that way and saw it, and told me. I'm mighty sorry, Hugh. It don't seem right to hit a man when he's down."

"I observe cattle tracks leadin' back from my water trough this way."

"That's another story," said Shadrow. "I won't deny some of my stock might've drifted yonder and used your water, the fence being down. But I will say that I figured you wouldn't like it, so I had the boys move such critters as was over there farther west."

"That was kind," murmured Hugh. He lighted his cigarette, studying Shadrow over the burning match tip. Shadrow grunted, tapping on the table again.

"Hugh, now that you're back what's up? Can't make any money on that ranch. You never did use it for anything but a place to sleep on occasionally. Want a job?"

"Doin' what?"

Shadrow's seamed cheeks displayed a little eagerness. "Write your own ticket. I'd rather have you on my payroll than any other man."

Hugh looked at Tolbert and said, amused, "That's no compliment to you, Lake."

Tolbert shifted his tobacco. "Accustomed to it by now."

"Leave Lake out of it," broke in the TS owner. "He's my shadow. Write your own ticket."

Hugh spoke straight from the shoulder. "You know damned well I never would work for you. And you know exactly why. So what's the reason for this mealy-mouthed offer?"

Shadrow's visage turned ironic and shrewd. "You never heard me ask any man to believe I did anything out of charity. I got my reasons for everything. Your privilege to figure there's a nigger in the woodpile. But you've got some chores to take care of, ain't you? That bein' so, you'll find it easier to do them wearin' a TS brand—with TS support behind you."

"What chores?"

"Don't make a dummy out of me," grunted Shadrow. "You

26

ain't goin' to have no luck startin' a private war. Throw in with me and I'll back you up on every play."

"Which means you figure I'm after somebody on the Testervis side."

"*I* didn't strip your place," said Shadrow.

"The offer is no good."

Shadrow squirmed in his chair and scowled. After a period of fretful silence he threw up his head. "All right. I make you another proposition. I'll buy your place."

"Why?"

"Wish you'd quit turnin' over boards to find the bugs underneath," grumbled Shadrow. "Don't you know why?"

"I've been away three months."

"Well, a lot's happened since then, Hugh. Right out, I'll tell you I could use the water you got."

"Sorry, not selling."

"That makes you out a fool," stated Shadrow, rising. "You won't be able to hold on. Somebody's going to get that water, whether you like it or not—and it might as well be me."

"Threat?"

"Hell, ain't I offerin' to pay for it?"

Hugh Tracy dropped the cigarette and ground it beneath a heel. He spoke coolly: "You're sayin' either you get it or the Testervis boys get it. I thought something like that, but I wanted to hear it straight. As far as you are concerned, you know what you can do."

"You're mad about it, not me," said Shadrow. "I made two straight propositions. Now I'll say this: There is going to be a fight in the Powder before thirty days is up. You've got to be on one side or the other—no straddlin'. And if you don't pick the right side, you ain't goin' to have any water. That is no threat. That's fact."

"You must want it pretty bad to offer to pay for it."

"I do," said Shadrow. "Cheapest way to get a thing is the way I want to get it. In this case it is cheaper to buy than to fight."

Hugh Tracy's square face chilled. "There is nothing I despise more than being told what I've got to do. I won't stand for it, Shadrow. Somebody tried to knock me over and didn't. Maybe it was a private affair and maybe it was just a part of this water business. I don't know, but I came back to find out. I'll find out, too. Nobody can hide his hand forever. And when I do, I'll do some shootin' on my own account."

"I didn't strip your place," Shadrow said again.

"For the time bein', we'll let it stand like that," replied Hugh.

"Nothin' stands as is," observed Shadrow sententiously. "But don't overestimate your strength. You're a white chip in a no-limit game."

Tracy didn't answer. Crossing the room, he walked to the porch. Shadrow made a surreptitious gesture at Tolbert and followed; and as Tracy reached his horse, the foreman also left the office and started slowly across the yard.

"My propositions stand—for a while," said Shadrow.

"You're talking to the wrong man," answered Hugh Tracy; and observing the foreman's move, he added quietly: "You know I can fight, Shadrow." Then he reined around and aimed into the mouth of the plaza. But he hadn't done a dozen yards before his wrist snapped a quick pressure on the reins. The blackness of sudden storm swept along his face, and the big body reared stiff in the saddle. Sid Maunders, lounging against a tool shed, faced him. Without looking around, he knew how completely he was cross-trapped. Shadrow was directly behind, Tolbert on his flank, Maunders in front.

"Come back, if you change your mind," called Shadrow, plain mockery in his words.

Maunder's full, flat-planed face glistened in the sunlight, and the opaque eyes clung steadily to Tracy. He was set, on a trigger tension, ready to react to the slightest warning. Expelling a breath, Tracy loosened the reins and rode by the gunman—out of the plaza and down the dusty road.

CHAPTER 4

···•◆•····

TURN OF THE SCREW

HUGH TRACY'S anger was of the slow-burning sort. Restless, skeptical, perplexed by a world in which he saw no plan, he clung the more rigidly to those few convictions he had. More than anybody else he understood that force was the universal instrument in this country, the court of first instance and last resort. Born and raised between the shadows of the two rearing rims, no man more clearly understood the dominating philosophy of the Powder desert. Yet the least hint of force applied in his direction was a chemical that produced explosion. And now, turning off the road and heading northerly homeward, his rebellious, unyielding temper reached a torch heat. Tade Shadrow had made a threat. Strip aside the vague blind of friendliness, the sly and evasive advice—it was nothing but a threat.

Nor was it spiritual balm to realize that, maneuvering him into a strategically weak location in the yard, those three men had thrown a fight in his face which he had been forced to refuse.

He was almost to his own ranch line before the full significance of that situation dawned on him. Obviously they were prepared to find him full of trouble. Preparedness meant, stripped down to the bare fact, fear. Fear of what, if not retaliation on his part for something they had done? According to that reasoning it was Tade Shadrow who had ordered the wrecking of his place; and since the act was but an after effect of his ambush, it followed Shadrow must have ordered the ambush too.

He struck his palm against the saddle so hard that the pony jumped. "But I will never be sure," he muttered. "It's done and over, covered up. All I can do is wait for a second try. It will come, sure enough. It's a game of waiting, with me on the wrong end."

One thing was certain: Powder desert, cockpit of dark antagonisms, was humming with the invisible warnings of another storm on the make. The days of surety and idle riding were gone. Once the sharp cleavage of faction was established, not one living soul in the country might say he was safe. So it had always been. That was feud. Thus thinking, he passed down the alley between pines and came out into his yard. Lynn Isherwood stood on the porch, waiting for him. "Had you stayed away another hour or so," she called, "I might have gotten something done."

Hugh chuckled, serenity unexpectedly returning to him. "Where's your rifle?"

"Hanging on the saddle of my horse."

He looked around. "So? Well, where's the horse?"

"In your barn, where it won't attract the inquisitive eye."

"Good girl!" he approved. "You know things."

"I was raised in the sagebrush. Should know something."

She was without a jacket this day, and the sleeves of her man's shirt were rolled up, exposing strong white arms in keeping with the slim, supple fingers. The ash-blonde hair was pulled back on her hatless head and up from her ears, disciplined by a tight knot in the rear. One smudge lay on a face flushed deeper than usual. The sober shadow he had noticed across her eyes the previous night was gone.

"Come inside and have a look. No matter what I did, I couldn't make it worse than it was."

He stepped to the porch and followed her through, stopping in surprise. He had not bothered, on rising that morning, to put things in shape. So all the orderliness confronting him was of her making. She had swept out the rooms, straightened the furniture; she had even pasted up the ripped wall paper and nailed back the frame of his bunk, upon which his blankets had been tucked and folded. Following her into the kitchen, the first thing he saw was the righted stove. That moved him to immediate question:

"How in thunder did you manage that?"

"Me and a two by four. And a piece of wood for a fulcrum. That's a good oven. I made a mess of biscuits in it."

"What with? All I could find around here this morning was a slab of bacon buried in the soot, and half a can of coffee."

He had never seen her laugh before. It changed the light of her eyes completely, made the clear and sharp face boyishly frank. "There's a story in that I won't mention now. It's noon, isn't it? I'm hungry."

"Wait a minute," said Hugh.

She turned back to him and sat on the table's edge, one leg swinging; sobered again and watching his face.

"Why?" asked Hugh.

"My manner of making apologies for shooting at you," she said.

"Trouble for you."

"If I like to do it, why complain?"

He shook his head. And it was entirely natural for him to say: "Lynn, don't let yourself in for anything."

The features of this girl were adaptable, quick-changing. She studied him, the straight glance clouded and touched by a half-startled expression. Sliding off the table, she swung toward the stove, answering over her slim shoulders, "Whatever I do, I don't regret. Perhaps I have also lived a little rough-and-tumble, Hugh. I can take care of myself. You saw me do it once, didn't you? Anyhow, we're going to have bacon and biscuits."

He turned and strolled outside, feeling some queer shift in himself. Whoever she was, wherever she came from, she colored her surroundings unmistakably. The challenge of her personality was direct and disturbing. Puzzled why this should be so, he heard her calling him back, and when he reached the kitchen he found she had in that short space of time produced a dinner of bacon and eggs, biscuits and coffee. The eggs brought him to a full halt.

"More mystery," said Lynn. "The less you ask about those eggs the better you'll like 'em."

There was no more talk for a time. They were both hungry and not ashamed to show it. But when the edge was off his appetite, he leaned back. "Resuming from where we stopped," said he, very slowly, "I'll have to say you are doing yourself no good being seen with me. From now on nobody in this country can afford to be a friend of mine."

"I know that."

He looked curiously at her. "I doubt if you do."

She leaned forward, putting her elbows on the table and cupping her chin between raised palms. "But I do. I could tell you something this minute, Hugh, that would make you flaming angry."

"Know about my temper, do you?"

"In the Antelope Hotel I saw the door you flung Bart Neal through."

"The worst of a man lives longest. All right. Then you know. Why risk coming here?"

"I gave you one reason—to make my apologies. Never press a woman for the literal truth."

He chuckled, big shoulders rising and squaring; amused lines formed around his mouth. "I'm not a good influence on little girls, Lynn. I don't believe in Santy Claus any more."

"You believe in many other things."

31

"Not enough. Not nearly enough. I've had a lot knocked out of me, and some pretty hard wisdom driven into me. If you fished around you wouldn't find such a lot."

"Trouble waters," said she, gray-blue eyes narrowing speculatively, "always make good fishing." They were finished and she got up, clearing the table. Slack in the chair, heavy fists lying loose before him, he watched her move gracefully and efficiently about the room. Thoughtfully silent, he curled a cigarette.

"Lynn, I'd like sometime to see you dressed as a woman."

She turned completely about, hands wet from dish water, and he thought it strange to find somberness deepening the light of her glance. "Must you think of me that way?"

"Of course," said Hugh Tracy, almost rough with the words. "No other way. And you'd be the last to want it any other way."

She dried her hands across her shirt front; her small square shoulders lifted in a slight shrug. "Maybe not." She moved by him, out to the porch. Following, he found her watching Mogul's rim with a troubled brow. "I was afraid of that, Hugh," she said. "I debated it before coming—and took the chance. But we'll swear off right here."

"What are you afraid of?"

"Not you. I'd never be afraid of you. It's something else. Will you get my horse?"

He walked to the barn, led back a small paint pony; and when he turned it in front of her he was broadly grinning. "So you picked a horse that didn't have a Powder country brand on it?"

She reached the saddle and smiled down at him. "I told you once I didn't want you to know where I live. I am practiced in deceit. So-long, Hugh. It was nice here—but I won't be coming back."

Hugh Tracy shook his head. "That sounds like an ending. But of the few hard lessons I have learned, this is one: Nothing ever ends."

"A fighter and a philosopher," mused the girl.

"Buckshot philosophy."

She leaned over, troubled and grave; one slim hand touched his shoulder. "They say you never avoid a fight—that you are too lucky to kill. For the next few weeks I hope with all my heart the first thing is wrong and the second right."

"So-long till next time."

Gathering the reins, she murmured, "There must not be a next time," and spurred toward the trees. Slouched against the porch

32

wall, he watched her straight, fine torso sway to the rhythm of the horse and at last vanish behind the pines. He dropped his cigarette in the dust and, climbing to his own saddle, turned up the slope to the northwest, bound for the Testervis ranch to ask the same question he had asked of Tade Shadrow. As he traveled, he had a premonition that suspended events were about to come crashing down around him. The very air held that surcharged feeling inevitably preceding storm.

Lynn Isherwood surmounted Mogul's plateau and wheeled to catch a last glance of Hugh Tracy. But the yard was empty and, slightly disappointed, she resumed her course. Pitching into one of the innumerable gullies that during wet season flung a lace-work of water over the sheer rim walls, she rose and instantly halted, right hand reaching for the rifle butt swung upward from the saddle horn. In front of her, no more than thirty feet away, a man spurred from an adjoining gully to bar her path.

Quick, flashing anger fired her face, pointed it more sharply. "I told you to keep out of my way," said the girl.

He was tall, with a loose and easy handsomeness of feature. Bold eyes laughed at her. "I risk my neck every time I come over this far," he drawled, "and this is all I get for it. Look here, honey, be reasonable with a man."

She swung the rifle around on its swivel, and the man revealed a sudden gust of irritation. "Yes, I know you'd shoot that damned thing. But don't try it. You tried last night—and I wasn't there, was I?"

She sat still, frowning at him; imperious, stormy-eyed. The man laughed again. "I saw the whole business. You thought I was down there and I wasn't. It was Tracy. You and him had quite a spell of conversation up here in the rimrock. I saw that, too."

"I thought I knew your kind pretty well," retorted the girl, "but spying on people makes a worse picture of it."

"You seem to get on with Hugh in fine style. That's goin' some for a stubborn fool like him."

"I notice that you didn't go to meet him."

"Why should I?" growled the man, passing back to anger. His moods played close to the surface. "I don't want anything of Tracy."

"Go on, ride away."

"You're not going to turn me off that easy," he said.

"You've tried your luck and it's no good," parried Lynn. "Now run."

33

He sat still, grinning at her. "I'm usually lucky in love, honey. What's the matter with my style? It ain't that you're modest about bein' alone with a man—not after makin' up Tracy's house for him."

She threw the gun muzzle on him, turned the safety. "You've stepped a little too far over the line, Bat Testervis. I will listen to no more of that talk!"

He folded his arms on the saddle and said slowly: "How would you like your uncle to know you came over to Tracy's ranch?"

"You wouldn't risk facing him."

"I can write, can't I?"

"Anonymous," said the girl, full of scorn. "Is there nothing in the whole catalogue of spite and meanness you won't try?"

A red tide went across his loose, blond features. "You've got a knack," he grumbled, "of getting me on the worst side. I'm not so bad. Put down that confounded gun and let me ride a little with you."

"Not a yard. Mosey along. I'm tired of going over this again."

His mouth snapped shut. Angry clear through, he jerked the horse around. "All right, you win another trick. But you can't get rid of me so easy. I'll keep ridin' across your trail till you give me a fair hearing."

She held the gun on him till he was a full two hundred yards away. Then, weariness showing through her eyes, she went on. Darkly she considered her situation. There was neither peace nor security in this land. Predatory and deceitful, Powder desert offered her no shelter, even in her own home. She could trust nobody. Nobody—and an odd current of mixed hope and despair ran through her as she thought of him—Hugh Tracy, a man she had met only twice in her life.

"I could trust him absolutely," she murmured. "Yet I have no business asking him for help. He is fighting for his own life now."

On Mogul's plateau, north of his house, Hugh Tracy crossed a rather deep arroyo at the edge of which stood a rock cairn marking the line between Shadow's outfit and the Testervis Double-O-on-a-Rail, _____ . The flat sweep of the rim began to break into low rolling ridges, isolated box buttes, and stands of pines. Incomparably the better cattle country, better grassed and better sheltered, it took a gently descending pitch, at last falling many miles beyond into that great flat bay of the prairie of which

34

Powder was but an indented finger. Accepting a well-defined road running easy gradients from one contour to another, Tracy settled to a steady lope, skirted the chrome face of a butte, and entered timber. A quarter-hour of this let him into the open again, between small bare ridges.

Certain things surprised him, made him more watchful. There was no stock grazing here where usually the Testervis boys ran heavy herds—that was one thing. And he was being watched. His first warning of this came in the shape of pony tracks cutting freshly into the dusty strip of road, preceding him a distance, and cutting out again. Closely attentive to the left-hand ridge, he thought he saw a peak of a hat slide behind a boulder. It was good rifle distance, and the memory of ambush still rankled; so without stopping, he reached for his own booted gun and laid it over the saddle. That act was immediately spotted. The yonder man rose from the rock and crossed both arms above his head, waving Hugh Tracy onward.

Tracy waved back. The two ridges joined ahead of him, and he pressed over this small summit, at once entering a country more broken and wooded. "Testervis scout," he reflected. If the game had come to this pass—stationed sentries, patrols, the whole preliminary skirmishing of uneasy truce—open war could not be far off. He met no more interruption in the succeeding five miles; but when a sharp circling road between the trees let him out upon a green, creek-sundered meadow in which the Testervis quarters pleasantly sat, two punchers appeared simultaneously from different angles and walked toward him. He crossed a flat plank bridge and faced these men, smiling slightly.

"Tracy," grunted one, deeply astonished. "Damn me, Hugh, I never thought y' would cut the mustard."

"Only way to kill me, Happy, is by throwin' me bodily over the rim."

"You'd only sprout wings and fly down," said the designated Happy.

"Don't make the angels mad. Where's brothers Morgan and Bat?"

Happy motioned to the porch, and Hugh rode forward. A middle-sized man dressed in neat black came through the door. Sober and quiet-speaking, he yet conveyed a sense of pleasure at seeing Hugh.

"I heard yesterday you'd come back. Light and rest. By Joe, I'm pleased."

Hugh slid from the saddle and went forward to seize the outstretched hand Morgan Testervis offered him. "You're the

35

first one that's said so. I'd sort of gathered I was bringing cholera into this country."

"Powder's changed," said Testervis. "Sit down."

He was a thoughtful man, this Morgan Testervis; around forty and quiet in manner and speech. As far removed from the average rawbone, decisive type of Westerner as it is possible to get, he would never have impressed any casual observer. He had a chubby face, slightly freckled; his eyes were brown and readily kind. The only dominating feature about him was a mouth that made one strong line across his face.

"I'd observed some difference," agreed Hugh.

"You're here," said Morgan Testervis, "to find out who wrecked your place."

"Good guess."

"First things first," observed Testervis, slowly. "You put most of your spare time on that ranch. Naturally it hurts to see the ruin. Good thing you wasn't runnin' any stock."

Hugh maintained silence, and after a while Testervis went quietly on: "I never lied to any man in my life. That miserable job is not of my doing."

"Your word is good with me, Morgan," said Hugh, looking around. The yard presented a different appearance than when he had last seen it. The changes were significant. A rack of rifles stood on the porch. Out by the creek two separate lines of cordwood, breast high, had been laid with some thought of presenting a barrier to the road. Lanes were cut through the surrounding trees at three different points, creating observation alleys to the hills beyond.

"Yes," murmured Testervis, seeing Tracy's glance go around the yard. "It's come to that. We're in a state of seige—or will be. I've got twenty men now who do nothing but stay around this house, waitin'. Maybe you've noticed already, but there's damned few riders to be seen in Antelope or on the desert."

Tracy nodded. Testervis went on: "One of three things has happened to 'em. They've pulled clear of the country, like wise men should. They've joined Shadrow, or they've enlisted with me."

"Morgan," asked Hugh, "Where's Bill Vivian?"

Testervis shook his head. "Ain't seen him a long time. Not since you got hit."

"He wouldn't run," said Hugh, shaking his head. "He never knew how. I don't get this sudden blow-up. Things are no different now than three months ago. What ticked off the grief?"

Testervis swung in his chair. "Take it for what it's worth. You're not listenin' to an impartial judge."

"Go ahead. Normally, you're peaceful. I don't think you started it."

"All right. The ball opened when you damned near got killed. That was no accident, Hugh. I will not essay to say who did it. I only say that two nights later your wire was cut and that a batch of cattle, not wearin' my brand, went into your water. Charley Sullivan, couple days after that, came to me and said he wanted a job. I gave it to him. He was sore about something. He rode line toward the boundary a week later—and that's where we found him. Dead. Not a hundred yards from your house."

"Tryin' to protect my place," said Hugh, invaded by a still rage. "Very well. That's the surface story. But it don't explain anything."

"Do you stop to realize that to either side of that rock boundary mark there's a good ten thousand acres not worth a nickel for grazin'—because it's got no water? Half is Shadrow's, half is mine. That is, we claim it for range when it really belongs to the government. But we don't use it because there ain't a single spring on it. Now think a minute. Where is closest water?"

"Mine."

"Sure." Testervis leaned forward and tapped Hugh's knee to emphasize his words. "And whoever gets your water has control of all that dry range. It's good for him—and nobody else. If I get your water, I've got ten thousand acres. My own plus the scope Shadrow claims. If he gets your water, he's winner. Figure it out for yourself—*I* didn't order you shot. I don't like range wars."

"If he wanted my water so bad, why didn't he offer to buy, long time ago?"

"Did you ever know of Shadrow payin' money for anything he could steal?" grunted Testervis. "He buried his own mother as a pauper to save a fifty-dollar casket."

Hugh shook his head. "I had that all figured out a long while back. But nothing ever happened my way, and I figured Shadrow wouldn't try it."

"Shadrow's one obsession is land," stated Testervis. "He'd wear his life away schemin' to get one bleak acre not fit to feed a horned toad. The reason he's let you alone till now is he's been busy consolidating himself south of Antelope. Well, that job is done. Shadrow owns all the Mogul from the Mica Buttes to my line. He owns three quarters of the desert—up to your spur. He's marched to that point. Now he's ready to march farther. Never forget, you're just one item——"

"I was called a white chip in a no-limit game by the gentleman this morning," interrupted Hugh.

"You saw him?" asked Testervis, a little surprised. "Well, he told you the truth. He wants your water for a foothold. He'll bring his cattle right down against me. He'll use your ridge as a convenient pass out of Mogul to the desert. He'll crowd my free range with stock until I'm starved out. At the first show of trouble on my part, he'll open up a fight, drive me clean off Mogul. And then he's got it all."

"He's not got it yet."

"You see me forted up, don't you?" commented Testervis, and raised his eyes across the creek to the high ground rolling down from the pines. A rider galloped full tilt into sight, rousing both the Testervis hands at the creek to sudden life; but when they saw him they wheeled into the shade again—and Morgan Testervis muttered some dissatisfied phrase under his breath.

Hugh grinned. "Bat travels like a shot out of a gun."

"No more sense than a louse on a hot brick," muttered Morgan.

Bat Testervis cantered across the yard, curiosity written across his loose, good-looking features. Identifying Hugh, his easy manner was replaced by a studied indifference. He wheeled, dismounted, squatted on the earth.

"See you're back, Tracy."

Hugh only nodded, not particularly astonished at the younger brother's lack of enthusiasm. Strong as iron, showy, jealous of his varied abilities, and loving popularity, Bat Testervis held a sort of arrogant resentment against Hugh Tracy for the latter's rough-and-tumble record in the Powder; once challenging Tracy's physical ability, he had met him at Indian wrestling and had been thrown severely on the flat of his back three times in succession. Never at any subsequent time had he been more than civil. At present, rolling a cigarette, he ignored Tracy.

"Where you been?" demanded Morgan.

"Oh, ridin' the south end."

"Just full of business that way lately," said the older man, glumly.

"What of it?" snapped Bat.

"One day you'll run into the Shadrow bunch and there'll be hell to pay. Maybe you're willing to start something, but you won't finish it. Use your head once in a while."

Bat blew smoke through his mouth and stared at his brother. "Stay home and knit socks, uh? I don't think much of your spunk. I've said before, and I'll repeat, there's no way out of this except to get every damned man together, go over there, and smash TS off the plateau."

"Or be smashed off."

"My God, where's your sand? Catch 'em when they ain't lookin'."

"I don't fight that way," said Morgan slowly.

"No. You'll sit here twiddlin' your thumbs till they come on the shoot."

"As long as I run this outfit," added Morgan, flattening each word, "I will handle things my style. A lot of men are going to get killed. I will not have the responsibility for that on my conscience."

Bat rose with an emphasized gesture of disgust, walking around the house. Morgan sat staring out into the lessening light of the late afternoon, glance slowly screwing up on some remote object. Tracy remained quiet, a little off ease at overhearing the disagreement, even though he knew this to be a common thing, and one of the weak points of the Testervis outfit. Morgan roused himself. "What are you going to do, Hugh?"

"He offered to buy," drawled Tracy. "I told him to forget it."

"What was his answer?"

"Plain enough. His declaration was that when trouble started I'd have to get on one side or the other, and that if I guessed the wrong side I was out of luck."

"And you will be."

"I know it," agreed Hugh. "But I will not buckle under to Tade Shadrow, Morgan. Not now, or ever."

Morgan Testervis stirred. "Listen. It's mighty disagreeable to say this—and I ain't forcin' your hand at all. You better sell out to me. You can't hold against him. I think I can. At any rate, singlehanded, you'll lose and I'll lose too—that water. Sounds cold-blooded, but it's war."

"In the morning I'm going to Antelope for a new bunch of wire. I'll string it. Next time Shadrow tries to cut it, we'll see. No, I won't sell."

"Didn't think you would," said Morgan regretfully.

Hugh Tracy rose, turned on Testervis. "But I'm in with you, Morgan."

Testervis jumped to his feet, moved by deep pleasure. "You are! Good—good! I wouldn't ask it, but I hoped mighty hard to hear you say it. Now, if there is anything you want, say so. Money, men——"

"You're in it that strong?" said Tracy, mildly surprised at the other man's show of sudden energy.

"Tracy, I'm no fighter. But nobody knows how much sweat and sorrow went into the making of this ranch. If Shadrow has his way, it's all wiped out and the Testervis family goes down. I will not let him do it. By God, I will not!''

"Lend me half a sack of grub,'' said Hugh. "I've got to get back before it's too dark. I don't care as much for starlight riding as I used to.''

Morgan Testervis nodded, passing inside the house. The sun was down, and twilight's transparency etched tree and slope in a bold relief. Through that evening hush the ranch sounds echoed, increasingly resonant. Men rose from odd angles and collected in the yard; the cook's triangle woke, its brassy "clang-clang" rolling out and up, shattering each far vista's huddled peace. Bat walked into sight again. "You're stickin' it out, Tracy?'' he asked, bluntly curious.

"Why not?'' countered Hugh, roiled by the man's half insolence.

Bat shrugged his shoulders. "You'll find most of your good friends have busted the breeze.''

"They'll be back.''

"I doubt it,'' contradicted Bat. He stared at Tracy, on the verge of saying something more. Instead, he turned off and stood on a porch step.

"You've got your fight,'' observed Tracy. "It'll be right under your nose.''

Bat laughed, short and sardonic. "My fight? Morgan's you mean. My way doesn't suit him. And if he gets us into a jam, he can struggle along by himself.''

Morgan came out, handing a half-filled gunnysack to Tracy. "Anything else?''

Hugh swung the sack over the saddle horn, mounted. "Not now. Listen, Morgan, you'd better keep a line of men strung out relay style toward my place.''

"Already done. You'll see them now and then.''

"So-long,'' said Tracy and cantered off. Across the bridge he looked back to find Morgan Testervis poised in the yard, a small and quiet figure full of worry.

The pines were aswirl with powder-colored shadows when Hugh entered them. Beyond, between the low ridges, full night caught him—a moonless night, broken by a crusted crystal starlight. Dimly, very dimly, he caught the moving bulk of a rider against the lesser darkness above the western ridge top; and the metal click of a horse's shoe flashed on rock. He guessed it to be the Testervis patrol keeping pace with him, and presently he lost the man altogether as he came upon the pitch gloom of another timbered mass. The sound of his travel ran ahead, full and free, breaking into the whorls and layers of separate echoes. But the velvet opacity around him was shelter. Merged with it, he made no target, and for a spell he let himself be swayed by that sense of wild, isolated freedom that was as much a part of him as the blood in his veins. This was his world, complete and satisfying. The beat of his pony was melody, the mingled dust and pine smell made a fine fragrance. In the deeps of the forest a bob-white launched his questioning, subdued whistle—human in accent.

But the mood passed when the trees dropped away and he entered the barrens. As distinctly as the broken lines of Mogul plateau stood out, so the joined silhouette of himself and the horse stood out. Alert now, unwinking, raking each deceptive pattern of darkness, he followed the bending road as it led away to his own place. The cairn stood somewhere on his right, westward. Solid objects seemed to move; and actually a whole strip of shadow shifted across his vision. Warned, nerves singing, he drew to a dead halt.

A line of riders appeared from a gully, not more than two hundred yards in advance, crossed the road, and continued on to the right. Swiftly estimating, he judged the party to be better than thirty strong; and while he watched, it faded into the broken area, beyond his view.

Sitting still, he debated his course rapidly. Without doubt those men were Shadrow's, for they came from TS soil; and Morgan Testervis had not spoken of putting one of his own parties out. The odd silence meant something more than a scout; the numbers indicated possible attack. Testervis had to be warned. There was no question of that; but it was a long ride back, and he faced the prospect of being treated as an intruder by the roaming Testervis sentries, one of which could not be far removed. The better idea was to break the quiet, put these men on guard. So, riding from the road into an adjacent ravine, he lifted his gun and fired once at the sky.

The immediate blast was like an explosion in the earth; and the succeeding echoes rolled on and on, flattening, swelling, and at last fainting into the far rim of the night. A deeper, more utter silence followed—that unnatural stillness in which even the night creatures cease to speak. But out of it presently rose the rush and pound of horsemen on the return. He saw their silhouettes again streaming across the black; and, crouched at the gully's lip, he felt the nearing tremble in the earth. They raced along the road—a smaller body of the main one, obviously—and swept

41

by. Northward a good distance he heard them swing off on a circle to rejoin the larger group.

He waited until the silence had drawn out. Then he pushed the horse from gully to gully and came to the spur of Mogul. That encounter had roused all of his suspicions, and he threaded the trees near his meadow some distance from the main trail. Reaching the clearing, he slipped to the ground and started forward. He had made some noise coming off Mogul and he knew that his own presence was advertised, if an ambush had been established. Not at all certain, but a little comforted by a lack of any intuitive warning—on which he strongly depended—he wheeled around the barn, explored it, and came to the house by the back side. He had a well-used trick for the occasion, which was to place one ear flat to the wall. Not the slightest sound indicated intrusion; and finally, dissatisfied by the creeping process, he crawled to the porch and threw himself into the doorway. Wheeling instantly aside and stiffening, he was met only by a further silence. Yet there had been somebody in the place, for the smell of cigarette smoke clung to the air. It took him half an hour to satisfy himself; afterwards he stabled the pony and rolled into his blankets for another night's half sleep and half watch.

CHAPTER 5

••••┅━━━◈━━━┅••••

THE BAITED MAN

AFTER breakfast, the flame of another hot August day spreading fanwise across the low east, Hugh Tracy cantered down the spur, Antelope-bound. All the way to the TS rim road it was an empty world; but at that point the mark of many pony hoofs lay on the earth and a fresh-disturbed dust still unsettled the crisp air; around a bend he viewed a compact body of horsemen preceding him some two miles at a fast clip.

In the wake of these, TS men undoubtedly, he thoughtfully revolved his chances through his mind. Never adept at fooling himself, and too long a citizen of the Powder to trust in the charity of his enemies, he definitely felt the danger of appearing in town. All it took now to produce an explosion was a chance word, a too-swift gesture of arm, some casual brush of shoulder against shoulder. Twenty-four hours previously he had thoroughly read Tade Shadrow, and he knew the added time would not have softened the man's purpose. Shadrow schemed too far ahead and too widely in extent to let the opposition of a single individual bother him greatly. His whole ruthless, contemptuous philosophy was expressed in that phrase clinging like a burr to Tracy's memory: "You're a white chip in a no-limit game."

The word was undoubtedly out amongst all the TS hands by now that it was open season on him. Given a chance, some one of that crew would try for him. Such was the blindly jealous spirit of paid partisans. There never had been much compunction of mercy in a Powder war; never would be. And if he was not prepared for the ultimate showdown, he had better turn back to the spur.

This was his reasoning as he racked along; carefully thought out to the issue—and then swept away. He would not go back.

There was never any ultimate sense avoiding a fight for the sake of a few days' preparation. His own headlong impulses disliked preparation, and this natural instinct to plunge on was fortified by the long knowledge of the country's way. Nothing ever reached climax by show stages. Uneasy peace held awhile, suppressing the underneath intrigues and deceits; the storm broke in full violence, sweeping aside all compacts and labored safeguards; peace came again for a while. The only thing that counted was an alertness, an instant readiness to ride the tempests. His own relaxed safeguards had brought ambush upon him. That mistake he meant never to repeat. And with this formed conviction, he rode into Antelope's northern end.

As he had suspected, Antelope was well-filled, strangely so for a Monday morning; and slowing to a walk, he ran a narrowed glance along the street. The weight of activity seemed to be at the other end, around the saloon and the courthouse adjoining. Most of the horses were racked there, and most of the crowd lounged or sauntered from one place to the other. His entry, he immediately discovered, created a quick shift of attention, and with deliberate forethought he rode to the mouth of the stable and left his horse at the rack there. It placed him more or less opposite the bulk of the TS men. But he halted only long enough to throw the reins over the pole, afterwards going directly to the hardware store.

He had known Ti MacGruder, the owner of that store, most of his life. Yet the reluctant "Hello, Hugh," had the distant civility of a stranger. In addition, there seemed to be a kind of appeal in MacGruder's eyes, possibly explained by a pair of punchers lounging near by as silent witnesses. Tracy nodded, playing the game MacGruder wanted because he understood the man's precarious position in this TS town.

"Two boxes of .45 shells," he said. When he got them and paid for them, he added: "Mac, I want about twenty spindles of barb-wire."

MacGruder showed surprise that turned rapidly to reluctance. Tracy saw his eyes flick over to the punchers and jerk back. "Bobwire? I don't know, Hugh. Don't think I got any."

"Yes, you have, Mac. Don't play freeze-out on me. Put 'em to the porch while I go hire a team and wagon off Jinks Bailey."

For some reason MacGruder's face relaxed and showed relief. "All right, Hugh. Get the wagon around and I'll roll the spindles out for you."

Tracy departed, catching the swift undertone of something said by the two TS hands. Across at the stable again he met the roustabout. "Where's Jinks?"

"Do' know."

"I want a team and wagon for today and tomorrow. Those two bays will do."

44

"Not on my say-so," said the roustabout slowly. "You'll have to see Jinks. I think I seed him go into Burkey's."

Tracy stared at the roustabout's evasive cheeks and pivoted about. The two hands in MacGruder's place were just now emerging, heading for the saloon. At that point the crowd had thinned during the short minutes since his arrival and he saw half a dozen hands casually scattered along the walks at the north end. Silently he said to himself: "It's here—right here," and the old, uncaring anger began to pump through him. He had no business going into Burkey's saloon, yet every man in this oppressive town understood the moves of the game as well as he did, and if he turned away from Antelope now it would be recognized instantly that he was retreating. So, squaring himself, he started out.

What stopped him, in the stable's archway, was the rapid approach of a man he knew—the sorrel Willy Bones. Bones saw him at the same time and checked back on his heels, raising a face stamped with worry.

"Tracy—hello, Tracy."

"Howdy, Bones."

Bones's lips went thin with pressure. He whipped a glance around him, pulled his shoulders together. "Tracy—you seen my horse?"

"No—just came in."

"It was here," muttered Bones. "By God, they got it!"

"Who got it?"

"It was right here," said Bones hurriedly, "when I went in for a drink. They got it. They don't want me to leave town!"

A fine, glistening film of sweat stood across his upper lip, and he pulled the lower one between his teeth. Both palms ran nervously up and down his coat. Hugh Tracy only half saw him, for the slow deploying of men along the street kept drawing his close attention. The in-and-out traffic at Burkey's door increased. One puncher left that porch and walked with an exaggerated straddle toward the stable, cool eyes pinned on Willy Bones's back. Up by the courthouse Tracy recognized Tade Shadrow's white saddle horse for the first time. "If you're a TS man," grunted Hugh, "why sweat about it?"

"I never ought to of come here," groaned Willy Bones. "Tracy, I went——"

The oncoming puncher called sharply, "Bones, let's go have a drink."

Willy Bones perked himself around, growing rigid. "Don't want a drink," he muttered.

"Sure you do," urged the puncher. "Sure you want a drink."

"Listen," snapped Bones, at once irritable and alarmed, "leave me alone."

The puncher came to a stand, pushed back his hat, and laid both palms on his hips. The cool, direct stare clung to Bones. "Look here, ain't I good enough to drink with? Don't come that proud stuff on me, Willy. You drinkin' or not?"

Bones stood very still, his back to Tracy. By and by his glance went creeping to either side of him. Afterwards he looked behind, and Tracy got the outright fear in the boy's eyes. It lasted only a moment. Bones said quietly, "All right, I'll come along."

"Fine," applauded the puncher in a casual, ironic voice. Never at any time during the interview had he glanced toward Tracy; and now he hooked his arm through Bones's elbow and led the youth across the street. Tracy let out a long breath. He didn't know what this was about, yet it was clear enough that TS was punishing one of its own members. Bones's expression of absolute fear was sufficient indication of it. Posted in the archway, Tracy's hardening inspection raked the idle groups of men situated here and there in the rising blaze of light. This grim play going on had suddenly assumed complexity. He wondered if Bones was bait dangled under his nose; and still wondering, he walked through the deep dust to the saloon side, brushed the body of a hand who stood in his path with an obvious arrogance, and entered Burkey's.

There was half a room of them, and they saw him the moment he pushed the doors aside. Bones, standing at the bar, drew back a little, a strong relief rushing across the set features. But it was of a moment's duration. Tracy could almost see this sorrel rider's thoughts go reasoning from hope to despair; and it was a plain gesture of defeat when the youth turned stolidly, blank-faced to the bar again, and swiftly reached for his whisky. If a man was afraid of the bullet's brief agony, Tracy thought a little contemptuously, drink was as good a drug as any. He stood in the middle of the room, the black lees of his temper staining the gray eyes to slate. One man's curse struck above the general confusion, to accent a slowly subsiding tone of talk. His traveling inspection reached behind the poker tables and stopped on the tall frame of Lake Tolbert.

Tolbert stood where he usually did, behind the crowd, off at a point of observation. His back was to a wall, the shackling body a little slouched. Wrapped in deep taciturnity as always, the impassive face registered no emotion, and the drooping lids closed out most of the expression of his eyes. Obviously he had watched Tracy from the moment of entry, for Tracy's glance instantly looked into the tall fellow's steady survey. Tolbert shifted his tobacco, swayed away from the wall.

"Mornin'."

Tracy nodded. "Hello, Lake."

"Drink?"

"Ain't that against your orders?" observed Hugh.

Tolbert let the phrase settle before answering. "It will make no difference in my fortunes—or yours," said he.

Tracy stared at the TS foreman. "At least that's an honest answer. I despise beatin' around the bush."

"Drink?" repeated Tolbert, and when he caught Tracy's slight nod he raised one slow arm and snapped his fingers. Tracy watched soberly, reading the foreman. This man had power, the power of silence and immovability and thoughtfulness. In that neat round head were ideas never unlocked; across those thin lips no unnecessary phrase had ever passed. An enigma to all, there was a touch of the sinister about him; and he was utterly obeyed. Lou Burkey hurried from the bar with a bottle and a pair of glasses, dividing a surreptitious glance between the two men. He lingered a moment, to be sent away by Tolbert's curt gesture. Tolbert filled the glasses, raised his own.

"I admire a stubborn man," said he, and drank. Twirling the empty glass around and around between his long, thin-ligamented fingers, he held the weight of his eyes on Tracy, and presently said: "Looking for somebody?"

"Jinks Bailey."

Tolbert nodded slightly. "To hire a team," he added. "You won't find Jinks. If you did, he wouldn't be rentin' teams."

"You know all the answers," grunted Tracy.

Tolbert's glance lifted against the gradually forming circle of men around him; and though there was no change on that angular, high-boned face, the circle dissolved. He returned his attention to Tracy. "You are a fool for bein' here today," he said, cool and remote.

"That's all you have to say?"

Tolbert ducked his head for a reply.

Hugh set down his glass. "Thanks for the drink," he murmured, and turned to the door. His mind seemed split into two separate cells, the one grasping every surface impression, the other slowly threshing at the edges of an increased question. Where, along the dragging, flat-footed marched of the moments, would the break come? Impatience gripped him, made a further rest in Burkey's impossible; the very air was surcharged with mass tension, with

47

the unspoken expectancy of every man around the room. He felt Tolbert's few words to be a part of the inevitable play, that they had served as a delay while other instruments of deceit came into line. Willy Bones clung to the bar, hat gone and his youthful face haggard. All this drove Tracy to the street. There were only three men on the porch now. Elsewhere the sentries were further scattered and lounging. One stood beneath the stable arch where none had been before. Looking that way, the set and rebellious cast of his face deepened. His horse was gone.

Poised, expecting anything in the space of a drawn breath, he felt the effect of some signal hidden from him. The nearest man on the porch wheeled, walked into Burkey's. A voice cut crisply through that inside silence

"Willy, let's go see if we can find that pony you been cryin' about."

The whole thing was a lie. Not yet knowing why, he understood TS was about to exercise its grisly vengefulness on Willy Bones. Willy knew it; every man in Antelope knew it. Willy had made no answer, but Hugh Tracy's ears got a deep, half-strangled intake of breath which could come only from the sorrel-faced puncher. The other man's voice broke more sharply into the singing silence. "All right. Let's go now." And presently there was the slow march of boots over Burkey's floor.

A feel of extreme urgency knotted his nerves, pushed him across the street to the stable's entrance. His horse, he instantly saw, stood at the back end of the place. But as he discovered it, the TS hand posted in the archway slowly pivoted to face him, deeply watchful, and he understood the man was there to block any chance of his reaching the animal. Tracy stopped, came about. On the street nobody moved; even the group at the courthouse ceased its shifting, and the hot sun flooded a town seemingly gripped by paralysis. Willy Bones stumbled out of Burkey's and turned indecisively from side to side. The escorting puncher came through, gripped his arm, led him toward the porch steps. Halfway across the dusty strip, a dull, strident voice stopped them both: "Bones, I want to see you."

What had been obscure was clear now; that familiar voice swept away all doubt. Sid Maunders walked into the edge of Tracy's vision from some hidden angle and advanced. Willy Bones wrenched free from the other puncher's retaining arm and took one long stride toward the stable. But only one, for he caught himself there; and as before, the intently watching Tracy could read very clearly the tumbling, despairing thoughts rioting through Willy Bones's head and arriving at the blank wall of futility. Making his stand, Bones straightened around and faced the oncoming Maunders. The other puncher, his part played out, slowly backed off.

Rage swelled in Tracy's throat. They were putting the kid under pressure—that cruel force so common in the Powder—and Willy Bones was showing the straight, fine grain of courage all the way through. This was TS business and so far none of his affair, yet his own position was bad, for what happened next would be as abrupt and immediate as a clap of thunder. Letting his big fists fall beside him, he turned on the TS sentry across the archway who so ceaselessly watched him. "Move out in the street."

The man showed surprise by the slight widening of his eyes. He shook his head.

"You'll have your turn later," snapped Hugh. "Get out of this stable."

The man's reply was a slow crooking of his elbows, a slight parting of his lips. Tracy, shrewdly guessing he could crack this fellow's nerves, ripped out another sentence: "The ball's about to open, and I'd as soon open it now. If anybody gets hurt it'll be you."

The other let out a breath, cursed slowly. "I'll go down the walk a few steps—not another inch."

"Go on!"

He walked toward the sentry. The latter, hamstrung by sudden doubt, grudgingly slid around the wall of the stable and backed away along the sidewalk. Tracy stopped where the other had been, his one flank at last safe. Sid Maunders marched on through the dust and finally halted at arm's length from Willy Bones, the enormous box-square torso dwarfing the youngster. His head tipped down a little, and across the flat-featured face lay the only expression he wore—that swart and unimaginative sullenness of one who lived in a starkly shadowed world. He thrust his hand outward.

"Shake, Willy."

As cold and blunt as that the trick was to be done. Tracy saw the trap open before him. Willy Bones remained rigid, nothing showing on his cheeks. Yet the strain of it corded his neck ligaments against the sorrel skin, and every muscle seemed to lock. Tracy balanced the alternatives in his head, just as he knew Willy Bones was doing. If the kid refused to shake, the quarrel was made and Maunders would snap at the chance; if the kid accepted that bruising paw, he would be tricked and killed. As cold and blunt as that it was to be done.

49

"What for?" asked Bones.

"I ain't seen you for a while," jeered Maunders.

"You been on my trail since I left TS," protested Bones. "And I been mindin' my own business strictly."

"Sure you have. You're a bright lad."

"Damn you," cried Bones, "leave me alone! It was a sorry day for me when I went to work for Tade Shadrow! I been cheated out of my wages, dogged around the hills and tracked like a wolf! All I want to do is to get out of this country!"

"Shake hands, Willy."

Tracy laid an iron grip on his impulses, yet even as he told himself to keep out of it and guard his own fortunes, he rapidly checked his position. On his left he was safe—being slightly inside the arch. Maunders was the only man directly in front. To his right a raking fire could reach him; and throwing a glance that way, he found Lake Tolbert lounging against a building wall across the street. Each part of the machine had slipped quietly into its place.

"My arm's gettin' tired, Bones," growled Maunders. "Shake."

Willy Bones swayed on his heels. Tracy, all at once proud of the kid, thought he had decided to refuse the hand and go down trying; and at that an overmastering impulse snapped the last fetter of caution.

"Take his hand, Willy," he snapped.

Willy Bones was at the breaking point, oscillating between purposes; the words drove into him and released the trigger set of his mind. Instantly, blindly, he seized the black fist stretched toward him. Maunders cursed out an enraged "Damn you!" and knocked the hand aside, throwing himself around at Tracy. Bracketed in the archway, Tracy knew then he had stepped into the trap prepared for him. But he was past caring, ridden by a savage desire to have the cards laid out for whatever they were worth. "Tracy," cried Maunders, "are you takin' up this quarrel?"

"It's what you wanted. Go ahead—make your try."

"Try? Damn you, I never try—I finish!"

"You didn't last time, Sid," said Tracy, the very calm of his manner biting into the deep, deep quiet.

"You lie, if——"

A shrill coyote yell burst like an alarm through the street, went wailing between the building walls. Maunders's teeth clamped down on an unspoken phrase. He threw back his head, and across the brutal pattern of his cheeks—never daring to leave Tracy—ran a straining attention. Every man within Tracy's vision went wheeling about to the northward. One puncher broke out of his tracks, ran a yard, and halted, uncertain. Somebody shouted: "No—not that way!" And Lake Tolbert's rearing body stood where it had been before, motionless.

"Vivian!" roared Tracy. Unnoticed, Willy Bones slowly edged into the stable and flattened himself behind a false angle of the arch, across from Tracy. Tracy yelled again. "Bill, stay where you are!"

"Ain't I?" cried an ironic voice. "Hell, ain't I? Tolbert, I got a bead on that bone rack of yours!"

"He's behind Overholt's!"

The uneasy puncher started to run again and was brought up by a command from Tolbert that was like the slash of a whip. "Stay put, you fool!"

A slack, sullen petulance deepened around Maunders's full lips; the hunting glint faded out of his eyes. Tracy, feeling the sway of fortune in each passing moment, knew that one climax had come and gone. The sure chance was lost—and Maunders was recoiling from pure gamble. The thing had been in this gunman's hands, safe and certain. Now that it no longer was so he was too cagey to let the responsibility remain with him. Both his arms relaxed, and quite slowly he turned his body toward Lake Tolbert. Nothing was said between them, but nothing could have been clearer than the unspoken question passed across to the TS foreman. Tolbert pushed himself away from the building wall. "All right," he said. "Show's over."

"Back up, Sid," ordered Tracy. "If you're all through, back up."

Tolbert's level, inscrutable glance came over to Tracy. "You're a lucky man, Hugh."

"Is that all?" grunted Tracy.

"I'm a poker player, too," replied Tolbert. "One of these days you'll draw to an inside straight—and lose."

A rider galloped through the line of poplars at a dead heat, out of the north, sending a call ahead: "Shadrow—where's Shadrow!" Then he saw Tolbert and bent down from the saddle. Something was said. Tolbert pointed toward the courthouse, smashed his palm against the pony's rump and sent it on. The tremendous calm of this TS foreman deserted him for once. Already on the run for his pony by the saloon, he rapped out a bomb-like order. "Stirrups—all of you!" Nothing more, but enough. The stationed punchers broke, dodging over the street. Maunders alone stood still, and Tolbert looked back and hailed him with a more incisive command. "Let the matter drop, Sid!" The messenger reached the head of the street, yelling for Shadrow again, and the turmoil increased. Maunders plunged into the confusion, thrusting others aside with his burly fists. Dust rose like smoke, and through it men's faces were a staring yellow. Riders and beasts fought for head room. Tolbert's agitated command faintly penetrated the mêlée. "Everybody up! I mean everybody. Maunders! Where are you?" Rail-straight in his saddle, Lake Tolbert reined to the middle of the street and laid his words about him as he would have used a quirt. "Get on—get on! Head north! Get on,—— damn you-all!" One wing and another of the party streamed raggedly by. Maunders wheeled beside the foreman, speaking to a deaf ear—for Tolbert was in cold rage and cursing at the laggards. Tade Shadrow spurred up, his thin, shrewd countenance full of excited energy. The others fell beside him and went away at dead tilt.

But Tracy, rooted in the archway, suddenly swore round and full. For another rider had come from the courthouse with Tade Shadrow and now rode abreast the three. It was Lynn Isherwood, and in passing Tracy she flashed a glance at him out of a dead white face; dark fear was in her eyes, but no recognition.

CHAPTER 6

···•···◆···•···

TRACY GUESSES WRONG

THE after-vacuum of their passage sucked the last dregs of vitality from Antelope. The town was empty, collapsed. High whorls of dust stretched all the way from courthouse to poplars, the sun burned down, water dripped monotonously into the stable trough—that was all. Tracy expelled a deep breath and stepped from the stable, his first move in ten long minutes.

"Crawl out, Bill."

An exultant whoop startled the uneasy echoes. Bill Vivian appeared from a between-buildings alleyway; not deliberately but in quick, cat-like strides, knees springing and his head turning from side to side as his glance went foraging about. He wore no hat, and a mop of unbelievably raw red hair tumbled about his skull. He was homely beyond the power to portray, all his features jarring with each other, and the whole effect was one of striking disharmony. Sun and wind had burned his face to mottled brick coloring; his eyes were a light and vivid green. Across an angular face deeply and vertically lined struck an exaggerated streak of a mouth. Small and thin, his movements were controlled by surges of impetuous nerves; and thus he came forward, yipping like an Indian.

"That time I paid for my keep, you son-of-a-gun!"

"It's a habit of yours to show up at the right minute," drawled Hugh. He gripped Vivian's hand, and they stood measuring each other over a prolonged silence. Vivian's mouth was stretched in a grotesque semicircular grin.

"Damn, you're a sight for sore eyes, Mister Tracy. But thin."

"And so he appears like a comet," reflected Hugh, "for a pop-eyed world to gaze upon."

"It took me an awful half-hour crawlin' up to this town."

"Looks to me like you been sleepin' in the trees ever since I left."

"That's truth. I left this country on the lope."

"As how?"

"After I took you to the hospital, I started back with the idea

53

of findin' out where that shot came from. Never made it. Couldn't get into the Powder with a box of dynamite. The beagles have been on my trail practically since the flood."

"TS?"

"You'd better believe it. Dogged me all over hell's acre and a half. Guess I've left empty shells in every dog hollow on Powder rim. A little birdie told me you was back, and I made a run acrost the desert. Got to your place last night and found you'd gone."

"So it was your tobacco smoke I smelled?"

"Ahuh. But I couldn't stay. Was somebody on my trail, and I figured if I didn't haul out sudden and draw this shadow with me you'd walk into him. Was on Mogul this mornin' and saw you slope for town. So I come."

"Where's the shadow?"

"I just got weary of bein' chaperoned. So I backtracked, slung down on the laddie, and tied him to a tree so hard he's practically part of the bark. Hope the ants bite him."

"And here we are," mused Tracy.

"Ain't we?" drawled Bill Vivian. "Hugh, you can't no more keep out of trouble than a magpie can keep from pickin' up strings. What in thunder ever possessed you to hit Antelope when it was full of Shadrow sports?"

"Came for barb-wire," said Tracy, staring past the poplars. "Bill, what made those mugs haul out of here so sudden?"

"Bobwire? You're goin' to refence and hold on?"

"The barb-wire is out. Changed my mind. But I'm holdin' on. Listen, there's only one thing that could put TS in such an awful sweat."

"Sure. Trouble with Testervis."

Tracy swung about. "We've got to get goin'. Bring your horse down here."

He went directly to the general store, bought a supply of grub and split it into two gunnysacks. Returning to the stable, he found not only Vivian ready for him but young Willy Bones also. Handing one of the sacks to the redhead, he shot a curious glance at the kid. "What for?"

Willy Bones spread his palms upward. "Where else could I go?"

"Hell-bent out of this country, which would be wise."

"No," said Willy doggedly. "That won't do. Shadrow owes me eighty dollars."

Hugh and Vivian swapped glances, and Vivian drawled an amused question: "Is that very damned important?"

"Anyhow, I'm ridin' with you fellows," said Willy, stubbornly insistent.

"Willy," broke in Hugh, "you'll be lucky to get out of it alive."

"Thunder, I was dead when I walked from Burkey's saloon. You can't kill a man more'n once."

"Better not," pressed Hugh.

Bones lifted a pair of concerned, begging eyes on Tracy. "I just got to. Doggone it, I just got to."

"Bill," said Hugh, "we've got an army. Let's go."

"You won't never regret it," cried Willy Bones; and, three abreast, they galloped out of Antelope. TS hoof dust strung a banner all along the foot of Mogul.

"I'm the only man in this party," said Bill Vivian, "that's got a lick of sense. You're pokin' your snoozer into bad medicine."

"I told Testervis I was throwin' in with him."

"With troubles of your own, you do that?" marveled Vivian.

"No way out of it."

"You can't cut the mustard this time, Hugh. They're too many."

"Counsel of caution from a man who never knew how to spell the word." This amiable bickering was like old times, and Hugh grinned, rolling his big shoulders forward. "All right, if we don't fight, what do we do?"

"We-ell," murmured Vivian, "from a judgmatical standpoint I'd say run. But I've tried runnin', and blast me it's awful hard work. So maybe you're right."

"I thought so."

Vivian covered his inconsistency with a bland expression, and the talk dropped. Twenty-Mile Rock was just ahead. Spurring off the road toward it, Tracy looked down at the surrounding dust and rejoined the others with a more sober face. "They didn't stop to water. That means hurry. Bill, somebody tipped over the apple cart up yonder on the plateau."

"Apple cart's always gettin' tipped over in this infernal country," growled Vivian.

Farther on, at the point where TS rim road climbed Mogul's fault, Hugh detoured again, seeking the story on the earth. But the risen dust was like a signal arrow along the desert road; Shadrow's men hadn't gone up the sharp climb. "Headin' through my place," observed Tracy shortly, and increased the pace. A change came over the party; there was no more talk. Willy Bones raked the foreground with his sharp, blue-eyed face, and Tracy, once casting an appraising glance at the youth, found no

55

sign of apprehension. The kid had grit. Somewhere in a short life he had been seasoned. As for Bill Vivian, that red-headed stormy petrel was a tower of strength. He was a fighter through and through; rash of talk and often impetuous in action, he yet understood when to play a cool, heady game. And there was no man in the Powder who so clearly knew all the devious devices and stratagems of sagebrush warfare.

The long road fled straightaway toward the foot slopes of the spur. Nothing breaking his thoughts, Tracy had time to wonder again about Lynn Isherwood. Her appearance with Shadrow had been a shock; and there followed now a whole train of puzzling queries. Considering her plain warning to him, he could see that she had never meant to deceive him. Whatever her position in the Shadrow scheme was, she thoroughly understood it. But the thing that kept returning to him, wherever his reasoning led, was the stamped fear visible on her cheeks as she had gone galloping out of Antelope. Deeper and deeper the mystery became, and of one thing he became increasingly sure: she was not happy in her place. Powder's arrogant force pressed on her too.

Bill Vivian spoke quietly—always a sign of that bantam's focused interest. "Hugh, they went through your place, all right."

"Straight on to the Testervis range, then," said Hugh. "Last night I saw around thirty men ridin' mighty quiet into the broken country."

"So that's what I heard," grunted Vivian. "There was a shot."

"Mine. I figured to warn the patrols Morgan Testervis had out. I believe——"

He stopped, canting his head aside. Out of the high distance a dwindling echo ran. One, spreading and vanishing. Vivian stared at Hugh, green eyes alive. "The ball opens," he murmured.

There was then a long lull in which the steady pound of their horses' hoofs and the squeal of their saddle leather strengthened. They reached the first climb of the spur, and as they did so, a long and ragged burst of firing rose from the higher horizon. "Not so far off," muttered Hugh and led the others into the pines.

"A little due care," warned Vivian.

Hugh charged around the last bend of the trail and reached the back of his house. Vivian promptly swung left to hit the other side, too old a hand at this sort of game to need prompting. Willy Bones, taking his cue, jumped from the saddle and went ducking and dodging toward the barn. Already on the ground,

56

Hugh took a quick glance through the side window of the house and found it empty. Thereupon he ran for the porch, to meet Vivian in full charge from the other side.

"They went on."

"Right through the yard," agreed Hugh.

Willy Bones trotted back from the barn. "She's empty."

Vivian winked at Hugh. "You'd think he done this all his born days."

Hugh lifted his head. The yonder firing had settled to a steady, detonating roll—somehow indicating a deadlocked affair. Weighing the sound, he guessed the point of trouble to be around the rock cairn, along the broken gullies where shelter was to be so easily had; fifty men, by the least reckoning, dug in and sniping away. Accustomed as he was to Powder's stormy history, the significance of what went on up there sobered him. The last pretense at legal method, the last vestigial remnant of orderliness, had been thrust aside. What happened now was open, bold. It was anarchy, the grimmest kind of survival by force.

Bill Vivian suddenly said: "Grass dies if you stand on it too long."

"We're going up there."

"I knew that. But why ponder at length?"

"Gettin' my conscience squared, maybe. Bill, you realize what's happening?"

Vivian's answer was a full and complete echo of himself. "Black's black. It's right or it's wrong. Don't clutter up your head with doubt or consideration. What's goin' to happen is goin' to happen. You're dead or you're alive."

"Willy," said Hugh, "you're sure you want to proceed? Nine miles straight across to the Powder rim and you're out of it."

"To live to a green old age and tell your grandchildren about a couple of tough mugs you once knew," drawled Vivian.

"Back up, Bill," grunted Hugh. "This ain't half so funny. Well, Willy?"

"What did I do that wasn't right?" complained Willy.

"Catamount's cub!" applauded Vivian, on the run for his horse; and Hugh made an accepting gesture of his arm. "I'm sorry, Willy. Come on."

The firing meanwhile had risen in pitch, vibrations crackling through the intense heat of the day. When they reached the trees and passed up the trail there was a momentary muffling of volume. But that was only the interim calm, the prelude to a fresh fury leaping into their faces once they arrived at the upper limit of the pines and stood in that arena-like space below the rim of the plateau. Each echo sailed over them flat and crisp. Beyond them, out of sight, roiling currents of sound eddied and reverberated. Even Vivian, casual and canny a fighter as he was, drew up his pony, to stare at Tracy with a face wholly absorbed by thoughtfulness.

"That's close," he muttered. "An' damn bitter."

Hugh paused only a moment, calculating the routes open. Then, pointing his pony at the rubble causeway—up which he had gone two nights before to find Lynn Isherwood—he raced forward.

"Watch out!" yelled Vivian. "Come back here!"

Tracy saw nothing above; but the urgency in his partner's voice was so great that he sheered off from the causeway and galloped into the pines, where the other two had gone. Vivian was on the ground. Rifle steadied beside a tree trunk, he watched the rim ahead. "Somebody's racin' for the trail, Hugh."

No sooner said than verified. Half a dozen horsemen swooped into sight, riding the very margin of the rim. At the causeway's upper end they came to a piled-up stop, studying the natural arena below; one of the group pointed. A rapped-out exclamation reached down.

"Shadrow's men all right," muttered Hugh. "Lookin' for trouble in this direction."

Vivian kicked over the rifle safety with his thumb. The fiddling restlessness so much a part of him had gone out, and he stood with his feet apart, bantam body relaxed against the tree, absolutely sure and confident. Willy Bones had picked another tree and watched Tracy in solemn attention. Hugh shook his head, studying the group above and listening to a fight that seemed now to fall away to a farther distance. It had lessened perceptibly in the passing moments, softened its tone. The shots came spaced and deliberate. Hearing all this, Tracy shook his head again with a profound and bitter sadness. He knew what the end was to be. Those clapping echoes of the fight were receding into Testervis country.

There was another indistinguishable murmur from the group above, and all of them wheeled and galloped away. Willy Bones, eager to do his part, started out of the timber and was next moment pinned in his tracks by Bill Vivian's swift negative.

"Why, ain't we——" stuttered the kid.

"You wait for the general's orders," reproved Bill. "They's two—three tricks in this game you ain't learned yet."

One long, reaching echo rolled over the rim; and afterwards a queer silence pulsed through the dead air layers. Hugh Tracy turned and stared at Vivian. "It's over, Bill."

Vivian had been reading the sounds, too. "Goodbye, Testervis."

"Yeah," muttered Hugh. "I bet on the wrong horse. Now we better go back to the house and wait for our spankin'. No—wait! Willy, pull your horse deeper into the bushes. Watch out, Bill!"

A single rider appeared on the rim and tipped down the causeway, hatless, flinging his quirt at every other jump. Hugh suddenly ran into the cleared area and waved his arm. "Happy, slow down!"

The rider flinched back in his saddle; then, recognizing Hugh, he rushed forward and literally threw the pony on its haunches. Sweat ran down his face like tears, and the thick dust lay in mottled patches on his cheeks.

"Happy, where's your outfit?" snapped Hugh.

"Gone!" yelled Happy. "Scattered to hell and gone! We got licked, Hugh!" The high breathing of the man turned to a choked spasm. There could be no doubt of it, this Happy was crying. "Watch for yourself, boys! We're through! Morgan Testervis is a-layin' dead up there with a bullet in his chest!" And he charged past them.

CHAPTER 7

···•──◆──•···

APPLIED FORCE

IT WAS one of the repeated ironies of Tollgate John Isherwood's rather sorry life that he should, the week before a not unexpected death in Nevada, consign his daughter, Lynn, to Tade Shadrow's "kindly and influential care" along with certain properties to be held by Tade in trusteeship until the girl was twenty-three years old. Having no faith at all in a woman's ability, Tollgate John had exercised the privilege of relationship and called on Shadrow, who was Lynn's uncle and only kin in the West. He never knew Shadrow's character, for it was in his lifetime a matter of pride that over in the vast reaches of southeast Oregon there lived one of the clan who controlled the resources of a small empire. He thought he had made admirable provisions; and so thinking, he turned his face to the wall with the first actual peace of his lifetime. Directly after his passing, not long following Hugh Tracy's ambush, Lynn Isherwood, with her roped trunk and her pleasant expectations, arrived at TS.

The first interview with this dissembling, avaricious man in the ramshackle desolation of that ranch house dispelled the pleasantness. She knew instantly there could be nothing kindly here. Within forty-eight hours she knew, too, that her life was pitched in a rough and violent and broadmouthed company. She was the only woman in a household through which hard, unscrupulous men tramped at any hour of the day or night. The treacheries, the whispered arguments, the whole round of Tade Shadrow's restless and conspiring activities came to her, even through the thin partitions of her room. A fighter herself, she had no weapons. All she could do was use a woman's patience and wait for some turn of events shadowed in the uncertain future. Soon enough realizing there was trouble afoot, it was the more strongly brought home to her when Shadrow one day peremptorily ordered her never to ride more than five miles from the quarters. This was oppressive, deadening, and there was no escape. Only once did she rebel. Shadrow, never a man to waste money, gave her the storeroom keys and in effect told her she was to be

60

housekeeper, cook, and general chatelaine. Under any other condition, she would have embraced the chance. Here, she knew what drudgery meant, and so she threw the keys in his face and rode her coal-black horse furiously out across the plateau, leaving her astonished uncle with a resentful knowledge that for once he was balked and could not enforce the law he laid down. Thus the situation stood.

She rode into Antelope that morning with the outfit, unaware of the developing trouble. Being in the courthouse, she missed the keyed-up scene developing around Tracy. But the call to arms brought her out and down the street, and she saw him then, at once comprehending his risk. Swept along by the party, she heard enough pass between her uncle and his two lieutenants to know what was ahead. At the rim road Shadrow curtly commanded her to go home; and accordingly she swung up the grade, watched the cavalcade race on, and in time reached the empty house.

Unpleasant enough when occupied, it seemed even more dismal empty. A sweltering heat invaded every room, powdered dust lay over everything. Contemplating flight often, she thought of it again, but rejected the idea quickly enough. Shadrow's long arm reached far out. Not a soul within fifty miles dared offer her shelter, and she knew too little of the land to risk a run-and-hide game.

Beyond dusk they came back, cantering easy style across the flats. Framed in the doorway, she watched them swing around the yard and dismount. Rough humor ran along the twilight. They seemed in high spirits, and she knew they had won. Even so, they had paid a price, for one hand led seven empty-saddled ponies toward the great barn. The group split toward the bunkhouses. Shadrow, the foreman, and Maunders came to the house, followed by another pair. Slipping back, Lynn went to her own room and closed the door, leaning against it. All her fear of this black place returned, and she felt indescribably alone, helpless. The men stamped into the office. Shadrow's grumbling seeped through the partition, and something fell to the floor.

Placed by the door, body rigid, it suddenly occurred to her that what they had done was only a part of what they would do; inevitably Hugh Tracy's fortunes came to her mind. And perhaps tonight her uncle might reveal his plans toward a man of whom he never bothered to conceal his dislike. Thinking of that, Lynn doubled one white fist and moved to the inner wall of the bedroom. They were speaking now, but the words were blurred.

61

All that came through the partition distinctly was a quick, harsh laugh. For a while she stood there; then, the risk of it leaving her a little breathless, she slipped to the door, opened and passed through it. The dark hall led out to a living room and thence to the porch. The other way it went toward an offset kitchen; and a little short of that was a right-angled corridor reaching another entry to the office. A sliver of light gushed through the bottom of the closed kitchen door, and she heard the cook banging pans on the stove; moving to the lesser corridor, she took three quick steps and crouched against the office door. Shadrow's desk was directly beyond it. She heard him talking.

"That's wrong, Sid. They're scattered all to hell, but they'll collect again."

Maunders's answering voice displayed impatience. "Then why didn't we follow and bust 'em up? Either you stop on what you've got or else you go do the job a second time."

"You're a fool at any sort of thinkin'," said Shadrow calmly. "Have a drink, boys."

They moved about, glasses tinkling against a bottle. A long pause followed, interrupted by Shadrow. "I never stop on what I've got. I never get enough and never will. You should know me better."

"Then we have to make another pitched fight of it?"

"One thing you need to learn, Sid. Let the other man move first and make his mistake. I was always mighty careful of Morgan Testervis, for he was a damned watchful fellow. But he's dead, see? And the rules we used on him ain't good any more."

Silence settled. Lynn heard her uncle breathing heavily. He moved around, chair squealing; and he resumed the thread of his thought. "They'll collect at the Testervis place. Of course they will. But it won't ever be the same ranch, don't forget that. About half of those duffers will skip the country. We've put the fear of God in 'em, you bet we have. So it's a weak ranch now. And it won't have Morgan to keep it goin'. He was the only one that counted. Put this in your hat. We can run our cattle five miles south of the cairn and never provoke a fight. They won't dare. We got that job done."

"And that's the extent of it?" asked one of the other punchers Lynn didn't know.

"I pay you thirty dollars a month," said Shadrow contemptuously, "and that's all you're worth. We're not finished with the job. We keep on goin'. But we wait to see what Bat Testervis does first. Ain't I said, wait out the other fellow? Well,

62

we won't have to wait long. Bat's a fool. Either he gets reckless and busts into a fight without any figurin' beforehand, or else he quits cold. You can't tell about him except to say whatever he does will be premature and flighty. Never was a lick of sense in him.''

Lake Tolbert's dead drawl came into the conversation for the first time. "You ain't completed this chore yet. There's Hugh Tracy.''

Maunders cursed. "The man's shot with luck! We had him and we lost him! Next time——''

Tolbert said: "I tell you something. Tracy's a bigger problem than the Testervis outfit right now.''

"Don't speak such damn nonsense!'' yelled Shadrow, suddenly touched on a sore spot.

"Tell you something more,'' went on Tolbert with that same down-pressing calm. "Miss him a third time and you'll never get him. Hugh's got no fear of any man that walks in pants. Be careful, Tade. He's your immediate business and will be till you salt him down. Leave him loose and you'll wake up one mornin' shot to pieces.''

"One man?'' scoffed Shadrow. "What's the matter with you, Tolbert?''

"A hunch. He's one man, sure. But he can get more scrappers together in a minute to fight you than anybody else could. This country takes Hugh for a winner.''

Lynn's heart leaped. Shadrow's chair banged violently against the door, and she heard him tramping back and forth, directly beyond it. Yet she clung to her place, waiting for something to come.

"If he had sense he'd be out of the valley now,'' growled Shadrow. "He ain't a fool. I told him what to expect.''

"And he laughed in your face,'' said Maunders, taking up Tolbert's line of thought. "There sure has been a mistake made, and I'm the man that is going to suffer for it. He's pointed at me. That misplay in Antelope was your fault, Tolbert. I had it worked right until you refused to give the high sign.''

"With Vivian layin' his sights on me? I like my skin.''

"And there's another trouble-maker,'' grunted Maunders. "Dammit, this business gets worse.''

"Where's Tracy apt to be now, Tolbert?'' demanded Shadrow.

"Unless I'm wrong,'' drawled Tolbert, "you'll find him on his place, forted up and waitin'. That's why I said you wasn't finished with this particular business yet.''

Shadrow's boots stamped into the wooden floor. Apparently

the chair was in his way, for it struck the door again so hard that the latch jumped out of its seat. Light gushed instantly through the widening aperture. Lynn's hand checked the door, and she wheeled silently back from certain discovery. So near had it been that she caught a momentary glance of her uncle's face—deeply lined and a fire-glow of anger in his eyes.

"Maunders," said he, "this is your fight. You've made a hash of it too many times. Get a dozen men and go back. If he's there, take care of him right. Burn the condemned place."

"Me again?" muttered the gunman. "How about Tolbert takin' a crack at it?"

"What do I pay *you* for?" challenged Shadrow.

The venom in the question stung the big-bodied lieutenant. He snapped back: "All right! I'll show you monkeys! But I'll stand for no more advice! Every time I been told how to do it. Now I'm goin' to go at it my way!"

"Fine," said Tolbert dryly.

The girl had enough. She backed down the short corridor and ran through the black hall as far as the living room. For a moment she stopped, exploring the dark shadows with her glance. Seeing nothing, she ran out a rear doorway and around the corner of the house. Maunders's square torso moved ahead of her, diagonally over the yard, and he was calling out the names of certain men in a fuming, arrogant voice.

Maunders she hated enough to shoot; but it was Lake Tolbert who inspired in her something far deeper—a dread, an actual creeping of the flesh. The man's eyes were blank. They denied light; they repulsed warmth or feeling. Yet this very impassivity spoke of inner emotions avariciously hoarded. And as she slowly crossed toward the small barn where Shadrow kept his own saddle horses, it was Tolbert she feared more than the dull, unimaginative Maunders. The foreman seemed to see everything, to have in his utter silence a comprehension of all that passed on TS. Thus it was with half relief and half apprehension that she reached the stable, groped in the dark for her pegged gear, and hastily saddled her favored coal-black. Leading him out a far end, she walked a good hundred yards onto the plateau before mounting. After that she drifted a like distance before clipping the animal with her heels. At this prompting the black went breasting away to the northwest, toward Hugh Tracy's place. The last thing she heard from the ranch was Maunders's heavy summons to his men.

* * *

64

The moment she entered the stable, Tolbert moved from an obscure angle of the porch and lifted a cupped cigarette to his mouth, turning his attention to Maunders out in the middle of the yard. He had seen the girl cross to the stable—the rest was obvious. Such was the mind of this foreman, grinding exceedingly small the acts and the words of those about him. One thing led to another, and all things answered to plan; there was no such phenomenon in the world as a meaningless act. He knew what others did or were likely to do because, long before the players fell to their parts, he had weighed them in the cold balance of his mind. Daily seeing them react, he understood what lures attracted them most surely, what impulses dominated their natures, what passions rode them hardest. Others spoke and revealed themselves. Tolbert locked himself in rigid silence and looked on. This night in the office he had stood at his usual place by the wall as a spectator rather than a performer; and, so placed, he saw Shadrow kick the chair into that near-by door, and he saw the door, flying open, suddenly recoil from a gentle pressure on the other side. Full of argument, none of the others caught that, but he did, and the gears of his brain instantly meshed and began a relentless revolving.

He guessed the girl might be hidden there to listen. She was the lone outlander on the ranch, the one rebel. Therefore, she would be the one person to do such a thing. Naturally, a desire to know what Shadrow was about had brought her to the risky position. But what fed that desire? No idle emotion, certainly. Profoundly shrewd as to people, Tolbert made another long guess. She had ridden the plateau considerably. She possibly had met Hugh Tracy. Indeed, he believed she had. Well, Tracy was a rebel, too; and these two people were young and healthy and attractive. The rest was simple. If she had spunk enough to listen in, she had spunk enough to convey what she heard. Tolbert never underestimated the fiber of Lynn Isherwood. All this pieced together, he stepped to the porch and drew back, placing his eyes on the spot where she was likely to appear if his reasoning was sound. She appeared there. It was that elementary.

What was not so elementary was the foreman's subsequent act. He remained on the porch until Maunders had gotten his men roused. Then, seeing the gunman tramp back to his horse by the main house, Tolbert shifted ahead and immediately caught the other's attention. Maunders motioned to the office and asked a subdued question. "Where's the old man?"

"Eatin'."

Maunders expelled a sharp blast of breath. "He's a foolin'

himself, Lake. He thinks we're goin' right ahead steamroller style. But I'm damned if we are. We've hit a snag. When thirty men can't handle three, it's time to do some thinkin'. I don't like it. They's a smell in the breeze. Call it a hunch, call it anything, but we've missed Hugh Tracy too many times. That——" and Maunders rolled out a guttural, descriptive oath. "He's pretty near bullet-proof. And I'm the man that's going to be hunted like a jackrabbit if he starts a snipin' contest."

Tolbert let the silence drag out. It was a trick of his, to build up suspense into which his words would fall with good effect. "Listen. Tracy's at his place."

"How in thunder do you know " challenged Maunders.

"Figure it out. Ever hear of Tracy runnin'? No. He'll scrap. Where will he scrap? At his ranch. So he's there."

"You're a long-headed cuss," said Maunders, grudging the approval.

"He's there. But if you try to sneak up from shelter you won't do anything but warn him. He won't be expectin' you to come— not after the hard day we've had. He'll be off guard. Go to the trees and bust out into his clearin' fast. Catch him sleepin'."

Maunders's suspicion, always half roused, came strongly to the fore. "Why this kindly advice, Lake?"

Tolbert drew a slow breath of smoke, expelled it. "Boggle this time, Sid, and Shadrow will land on you with both feet. He's pretty sore about Tracy."

It was Maunders's turn to remain silent. He came a little closer, peering up at the foreman's obscure cheeks, trying to catch some telltale expression. But it was futile, and he fell to surreptitious talk.

"You don't fool me, Tolbert. You ain't workin' here for love—no more than me. What's up your sleeve?"

"What would be?" parried Tolbert, expressionless.

"I dunno. Can't see the cards you're playin'. But, brother, I know damn well you're playin' 'em. Let a man in the game, Lake."

"Poppycock."

"Lone hand, uh?" muttered Maunders. "Well, I didn't think you'd be that foolish. Don't you know it's what Shadrow wants— you and me pullin' apart? He never lied when he said you was to watch me and I was to watch you. Get wise to it."

"Don't try to cross him, Sid. Can't be done."

"You're a fool," said Maunders.

"Wiser than you. I know my limits, and I know Shadrow. He's got us both watched all the time."

Maunders pivoted his big body, staring into the shadows. After that he climbed to his horse and reined around. Tolbert emitted a soft warning. "Don't creep up. Bust down there—and you better not make a foozle of it this time."

Maunders galloped away, drawing his men behind. Tolbert had detained him a good ten minutes behind Lynn Isherwood. Tolbert had lied to him about Tracy's unpreparedness—for Tracy would be prepared. In that small round head of the foreman a thought flipped over and found its place. Pinching out his smoke, he went to the mess hall, thawing to a reserved affability during the meal.

Lynn knew the road well, and the coal-black went along it at an unchecked pace. Once the never-quite-absent fear of Shadrow's vengeful power so startled her that she stopped dead and listened. But nothing came out of the long sweep of night save the far-off ululating chant of a coyote; and after it died there was only the gentle run of the western wind. Of the darkness itself she had no apprehensions. This was her kind of country, and she loved it. The isolation, the long distances, the raw flame of day, and the mystery of the star-swept heavens overhead—these bold contrasts and this generous amplitude made up a world of supreme wonders. Born into it, she could conceive no other as satisfying. It was a splendid world—out-flung, majestic, beautiful in its own barbaric style; and even in the league upon league of utterly barren range, where water was not and life could not exist, and upon which the full swelter of the sun lifted mirage after mirage, she saw the mark of prodigal beauty. Another might come here and stand oppressed by the actual desolation; it never occurred to her that this was desolation. There was a deep, profound rhythm to the land, and she felt it.

For a while she half forgot the trouble that had put her on the road. But it came back to her as she drew into the rough surfaces of Mogul near the spur. She found the trail leading down toward Tracy's after slow exploration, and at the tree line she pulled the pony to a slow drift. No sound came from behind; no light winked out of the house ahead, and a heavy sensation of discouragement passed through her. To see Hugh, if only for a moment, meant some lightening of her load, some break in the long monotony; it was compensation for the risk of Tade Shadrow's evil temper when she returned to face him. Considerably let down, she halted at the edge of the meadow and dropped a soft call into the stillness:

"Hugh."

The answer was immediate, enormously heartening. Hugh's voice struck out of an angle by the barn. "Easy, boys. Lynn, what in thunder——" She heard him running across the yard. Going on, she saw the solid outline of the man appear beside her horse. A hand reached up, gripped her arm. She stepped down.

"What did you come for?" said Hugh.

"Maunders is on the way with some men—about a dozen, I think."

"How do you know?"

"I overheard Tade tell him."

"And you risked it?" muttered Hugh. The concern and anger of his words furnished her with an odd sense of happiness. "Lynn, I've got enough on my conscience without adding any more. Don't you know what Shadrow will do to you?"

"He'll only think I've been roaming. He's used to it."

"But if he finds out——" muttered Tracy and stopped. After a while he called back: "Bill, did you hear that?"

"Ahuh."

"Everybody I touch gets into grief," rumbled Tracy. "You can't stay, but if you go back you're not safe."

She had made her own decisions for so long, and she had been friendless for so long, that it was like luxury to stand idle and hear Tracy shoulder her problems. Yet it was a forbidden luxury, and she recalled herself with a small sense of guilt. "No, I'm going back. He won't find out. He could do nothing if he did."

"In the first place, how did you get on that ranch?"

She told him in swift, brief phrases. Tracy said: "He's your trustee? That wolf? What kind of a world is it when such things are allowed to be? Lynn, is there no other place you can go?"

"None, Hugh."

"Foolish question on my part. You couldn't get away now anyhow."

She caught the upthrust of his glowering rebellion, and once more that little sense of guilty happiness came to color the night and its trickeries.

"I can't do a thing," muttered Tracy. "Not a thing! Lynn, it's a damnable pass! There is no shelter here for you. Not a bit of safety anywhere around me."

"I'm going back. Don't worry about it, Hugh. He will discover nothing."

"That wolf," grunted Tracy. "He's a bloody man, Lynn. Today he killed off Morgan Testervis, who was a thousand times better than Tade ever will be. He's broken down all opposition."

"Except us," came a dry voice from the darkness.

68

"Except us," repeated Hugh slowly.

"What are you going to do?" demanded Lynn. "Not stay? Oh, no! You aren't able to do that. Tade fears you. Tolbert told him nothing was settled until you were out of the way. You see? He won't stop until he has you. It's impossible to hold against him."

"Impossible," came Bill Vivian's casual voice, "is a funny word. Come to study it close and what do you find? Why, that most of the darned thing is 'possible.' "

"Time's goin'," said Hugh. "When you get to the top of the trees, Lynn, take the causeway and swing wide of the trail."

"Hugh," said the girl wistfully. All their meetings came to such abrupt ends. Never was there a promise of a next time, least of all now. She wanted to say something and didn't know what it was to be. But Tracy, pressed by anxiety, took her arm, urged her back to the saddle. Sitting there, she caught the black mass of his hair and the square lines of the tilted features.

"If you've got to run away," said Hugh quickly, "remember this. Follow the Testervis road beyond the rock cairn. As far as the first heavy stand of pines. Swing off the road when you hit the trees—swing to your left and keep going until you come to a quarried-out clearing. I'll try to make it every few days. You've got to hustle now, Lynn."

She wanted to make it a cheerful good-bye. But what she said was, "I don't see anything but defeat for us, Hugh! Oh, be so careful!" The grip of his palm increased and fell away, and she spurred into the timber. All the buoying power of his presence ended, the trees were abysmally black. Suddenly and overwhelmingly afraid, she lashed the black and pounded up to the arena. The horse swung toward the fissure trail, resisting her rein pressure. When she fought him to the causeway, the charge of his hoofs lifted great eddies of sound, and it seemed as if all the world could hear. Half in panic, she arrived at Mogul's surface and plunged into the dark emptiness. A quarter-mile beyond the road she halted.

Maunders was out there, passing by. Soft repercussions crossed the flat and faded. There was, afterwards, no sound at all. Lynn gripped the reins and listened with a straining attention, every impulse holding her to the spot until some inkling of Tracy's fortune was borne back. But TS and the inevitable scene with Shadrow was something she dared not longer postpone. So, curling to the road, she set out at a gallop. Long afterwards there was some firing behind, damped by the distance. She counted two distinct bursts and a ragged after-volley. Then silence came, and she urged the horse to a faster gait, afraid now that Maunders might return and overtake her.

The girl gone, Hugh strode into the house and lighted a lamp, placing it before a window. After that, he returned to the yard and paused a moment by Bill Vivian, whose station was behind a porch end. Willy Bones, troubled about something, called from the barn: "Anything up?"

"Wait it out, Willy. And no more talkin'. Don't leave your place, no matter what happens."

Bill Vivian rose from a crouch and stamped his feet on the dirt. "Women," said he, softly, "constitute a large portion of the globe. But what of it? So does sagebrush. Ain't we got enough to unscramble as is?"

"He's a wolf," muttered Tracy, thinking of Shadrow. "It's a rotten universe and no order in it when a thing like that can happen. A trustee for that girl—imagine it, Bill."

Vivian never troubled himself with reflection. "Never mind the universe, Hugh. It's the bow-legged ants which are men so-called that make all the grief."

Hugh whirled and headed for the water trough on the run, some faint alarm in the trees coming to him. He reached the trough and seized the rifle standing beside it. Vivian's gun lock clicked through a dead stillness that was the next moment burst apart by a slashing of brush and the rolling stampede of hoofs. They came out of the trees in a breasting line, their shadows cleaving the mass of night; and they came in full voice. Maunders yelled, that strident and arrogant tone recognizable anywhere. Two streaming points wedged into the clearing, one racing for the house, the other swinging wide of the water trough. Hugh Tracy, throwing up his rifle, smashed a bullet into a down-bearing figure and saw the man flinch. The yelling ceased instantly, and all the yard shuddered with a concerted firing. His target fell, the horse raced riderless by. Another target came on, boiling up the water of the trough with one shot and another. Utterly cold, Tracy caught the man no more than ten feet away, caught him solidly in the body. Willy Bones was shouting from the barn, and over there a recoiling fringe of Maunders's riders drummed the boards with a hot volleying. Worried—and free of attack at that moment—Tracy swung about and raked the agitated darkness by that structure. Something smashed against the house behind him, but Vivian was holding fast and he had no concern. A horseman galloped out of the mass by the barn,

70

wheeled and charged straight for Tracy. A jet of muzzle fire bloomed in his face and the wash of the bullet stung his cheek in passing by. Willy Bones cried again, openly defiant. But as suddenly as it had started, it was over; no more rush and pound behind him, no more weaving bodies ahead. Turning a complete circle, he saw nothing upon which to pin a shot. There were a whipping and a crushing of brush and a final retort from one gun; then the beat of hoofs died into the upper slopes, and silence rushed in.

"Bill," snapped Hugh. "Willy."

He heard Willy swearing in a pleased way; and Vivian's drawl reached him—relieving a quick apprehension. "How about it, Mister Tracy?" said Bill. "Ever know of the time when a good little man couldn't lick a good big one?"

Tracy paced slowly toward the house. "It's the first open fight, Bill. And we were lucky, breakin' even."

"Even?" protested Bill Vivian. "We drove 'em off, didn't we?"

"We drove 'em off, but they win the place. That's even."

"What kind of arithmetic you usin'?" grumbled Vivian.

"They'll come again. Next time all of TS will be here. Next time they can have it. From now on, Bill, this is a run-and-jump affair. Come on—we move out."

Vivian grumbled but said nothing. He had always accepted Hugh's leadership without question, and he did so now. Five minutes later the three of them were riding single file through the trees. Scouting the arena carefully, they pulled to the top of Mogul's rim, and at that point Hugh curved to the northeast, passed the rock cairn, and led away into the hidden reaches of the night; saying nothing, full of heavy and rebellious thoughts.

Bill said: "What's life but a lease on somethin' which ain't permanent nohow? Me, I'm so far behind in my rent that any time I cash in now I win."

CHAPTER 8

LOOSE ENDS

BILL VIVIAN drank a little cold coffee out of the common can and wiped the beaded sweat from his face. "Somebody," he grumbled, "says an empty stomach makes a clear head for thinkin'. But what fool would bother about thinkin' in a dumb country like this?"

From the ridge on which they were hidden, Mogul's tawny floor lay visible east and west, throwing up heat whorls all the day through. South, a bay of pines shut out whatever went on around the spur; and to the north, where lay the Testervis ranch, the low hills closed the horizon. Flat on his stomach, Hugh Tracy watched the edges of distance. Throughout the morning nothing happened; shortly afterwards the slow, fugitive shift of some developing play began to make appearance. About one o'clock a long banner of dust appeared over on TS territory, rolled heavily, and subsided. For a long while the burning glare yonder remained unbroken; but around three a steady point showed upon the TS road, throwing a still thicker dust fog above, and presently Tracy recognized the advance of a considerable body of cattle. In another hour the driven herd swung to the east and the intervening trees shut it from sight; but he knew Shadrow's occupation of the spur had at last taken place.

Vivian, looking on, made his irritated observations. "And all our bustin' around the landscape don't help us none. Cattle, travelin' about three miles an hour, is the most permanent thing I know of. The steam roller bears down, Hugh."

Tracy only nodded, for his ranging glance, not satisfied, passed to the west. Something went on there as well. One rider struck out of an arroyo and took up a rising and falling advance, utilizing each low area he came upon. Still farther westward a thin blur broke the brassy shield of light, stood suspended against it a moment, and vanished. Meanwhile, the nearer rider disappeared.

"Shadrow," opined Bill Vivian, "is goin' to take another hack at the Testervis bunch."

Willy Bones said, "Look here," from the opposite side of the depression—almost the only words he had spoken during the day. Tracy and Vivian walked across the bowl together and lifted themselves to the edge. Half a dozen riders came along the Testervis road, appeared directly beneath the watchers, and plunged into the southerly trees.

"On the scout," guessed Vivian. "And they'll come back twice as fast when they see that herd."

He was mistaken. A long, dragging hour passed, and beyond six the sun plunged from sight with all the smoky fury of a molten body striking water. Twilight arrived, washing across the land in long runnels of gray and steel-blue color. The distance was empty of movement—and the Testervis hands made no reappearance. Tracy turned from the edge of the depression.

"You waited all day," said Vivian, "and what for?"

"For a break we might use," answered Tracy.

"None came."

"None came," agreed Tracy. "You know what sort of a fight we have to make, don't you?"

"Sure. Bite 'em on the tail and run like the devil."

"Exactly."

"Providin'," amended Vivian, "we ever get close enough to do any bitin'. Shadrow knows what we're up against. He'll see we don't get any chance to operate."

"He's got a young army," said Tracy, eyes half closed. "All of them just paid hands. Ever hear of a paid hand riskin' his hide when he couldn't see the profit in it?"

Vivian's eyes lighted, and he chuckled. "Snipe 'em—scare 'em—make 'em wonder where the next shot's comin' from. Now you're talkin'. Move around. Do somethin'."

"That's half of it. Shadrow's no man to make his crew fight out of loyalty. If we could put the fear of ambush, day and night and any time at all, into the heads of those mugs, they'd start runnin'."

"Agreed," said Vivian heartily. "So we will, says old man Vivian's little boy Bill."

"Back up," grunted Hugh. "You forget something."

"Listen. Don't lay any mature and deliberate plans, Mister Tracy. It won't work. Nothin' in this condemned scope of alkali and loco-weed stays put long enough to hook a plan on. You figure somethin' out and blooey the next minute your figgerin' is all wrong. You stick your thumb on a situation, and by gosh it ain't there when you look second time. No. Any sort of a plan's

73

no good. Best thing to do is take what comes and hack at it. Then run and wait for somethin' else.''

Tracy shook his head. "There's another side to the story. Three men on that ranch we can't scare. Take all the pot shots we want, do all the ridin' we want—Shadrow and his two blackjacks are still squattin' right where they always squatted. Nothing changes till they change.''

"All right," said Vivian, impatient at such logic. "What's the answer?''

"Wait for a break.''

"We done it all day long. See a break yet? I don't.''

"Or make one," added Hugh quietly.

Vivian turned a squint-eyed regard on Tracy. "You got some stunt in your coco," he accused. "What is it?''

Tracy shrugged his big shoulders. "Don't know. But right now I'm going over to see what the Testervis layout is. You boys stay here. We can't afford to put all our eggs in one basket.''

Vivian grinned again. "The eggs wouldn't bust. They're hard-boiled.'' When Hugh got his horse and started out of the depression, he added: "Bring back half a cow barbecued. I grunt much better on a full stomach.''

Tracy went through the last of the twilight and into an enveloping nightfall. A half-mile farther along the ridge he quartered down to the road, breasted a slight summit, and proceeded through a darkling alley between pines. Testervis ranch quarters were not much more than half an hour's quick run ahead, and he let the pony stretch after the tedium of a day's waiting. As for himself, the freedom of the saddle was a tonic for the dammed-up restlessness in him. Like Vivian, he could not help chafing at delay. He was not a man blessed by much patience, and when, as at present, the tide of luck ran out it was nothing less than punishment to withdraw from the only sure course of action he understood, which was to strike back—risk his fortunes and strike back. Yet, unsettled and mordant as his temper was, he knew Shadrow to be a shrewd and unforgiving enemy; an enemy with patience and cunning and enormous power. He could not throw himself against this unyielding wall; he had to find a breach in it.

He could see no breach now, nor reason his way through to a situation where one might logically exist. It seemed to him, in fact, that the game had come to a deadlock. Shadrow could not find him; he could not touch Shadrow. And as time passed, he, Tracy, lost ground.

74

"Even now," concluded Tracy, "with nothing much to fear and almost everything won, he will take no chances. Each advance he makes will be supported, well defended."

The road curved out of the trees and ran along a straight stretch before reaching another pine stand. Directly beyond that was the Testervis place, and Hugh, knowing it would be guarded, swung from the road and picked a careful route roundabout. He watched for the glimmer of house lights, but he saw none; not even when he drifted down a slope and halted at the margin of the yard. Nothing moved, nor was there any rumor of activity. Always ready to ride, the Testervis bunch usually kept a string of saddled stock by the porch or by the corral, but as his eyes adjusted themselves and reached to either location he found no sign of horses.

For a long while he rested there, puzzled and alert—waiting for some telltale signal to cross the stillness. After a full ten minutes had passed fruitlessly by, he chanced a soft challenge:

"Hello, house."

The echoes came back into his face, and he realized then that as surely as Morgan Testervis was dead, so was the Double-O-on-a-Rail. Headquarters had been abandoned.

He had no further curiosity. Turning, he retreated to the road and went away at a steady gallop. What happened to the Testervis hands he didn't know. What Bat's plan might be he couldn't fathom, nor would he attempt to. It was sufficient knowledge that the blond brother, throwing aside Morgan's entrenched determination never to let the fight go back of home quarters, had abandoned the place. It was a certain augury, and one small article of hope in Hugh's head ceased to be important. The TS tide would come rolling down, pause here, and sweep on to the very limit of the Mogul plateau. If that house, symbol of ownership, wasn't worth fighting for, then nothing was. Around no other point would Bat ever be able to rally his men.

The road was in deeper darkness when Hugh left it and climbed the bald ridge. A little uncertain of the footing, he sidled across the spine of the high ground and about fifty yards from the depression sent out a subdued hail. Evoking no reply, he pressed on and entered the hideout.

"Bill."

The word sank like a plummet into the stillness. Suddenly alarmed, he stepped to the ground and walked the whole length of the depression. It was quite empty.

For a while he stood in his tracks, puzzling out this added change. Need of water might have taken the men down the slope to a spring near the pines; Testervis men passing by might have drawn them from concealment; or the proximity of TS parties might either have alarmed them or suggested the chance of a coup. But if it had been water, one would have remained behind while the other went away. There remained, then, the possibility of TS men in the neighborhood. Turning, he crouched against the earth, listening for whatever chance rumors might come over the rim.

It was a futile wait. But it was also a switching point in all his calculations. During this long day there had been a great and growing uneasiness that now, given the chance to crystallize, usurped every other consideration. Once having thought to do something, Hugh never dallied. Reaching into his pocket for a scrap of paper and a pencil, he wrote a message there in the sightless dark:

"Tomorrow morning."

He made it no plainer, afraid of some alien eye discovering it; and he laid it beneath a rock, one edge in view as nearly as he could make out. Returning to his horse, he rode from the depression.

"This scattering process," he said to himself, "has about reached its conclusion. I'm left by myself."

Angling down the ridge, he quietly entered the trees and made a detour through them to that quarried-out place he had described to Lynn Isherwood. But he found nothing there—had hoped for nothing as a matter of fact; and he left it, satisfied that his back trail was clear. More or less, he was squaring his conscience for what lay ahead. Beyond the trees, he pointed into the due south and went rapidly on. Once, at the very edge of Mogul's rim, he looked down and saw the lights of his house burning and a lantern bobbing across the yard.

Lynn Isherwood had reached TS quarters the previous night without discovery and, supperless, went to bed. At any moment expecting to have Shadrow call her out, she at last fell into so deep a sleep that she never heard Maunders storm back, never heard the wild echoes coming from Shadrow's office. Next morning she woke late, eating after the others had finished; Shadrow was gone, with his lieutenants and his crew. But a man sat idly by the small barn, casting loose loops at two prongs of wood stuck in a hay bale, and she knew, without testing her knowledge, what he was for. The day dragged. There was nothing to do but turn up the old thoughts and suppress the old apprehensions. In front of a window she stared. across Mogul's barren flat toward Hugh Tracy's, wondering what had happened to him. Supper was late that night, for it was beyond dusk when Shadrow and the outfit returned; and though she sat at the table with them, she heard no news. They were far more silent than usual. Shadrow said nothing at all, but from time to time she felt his eyes on her. It was a long-drawn-out ordeal, short as that meal was. Afterwards she went to her room, suddenly and profoundly fearful.

Shadrow had gone to his office. Through the partition she caught the mingling of voices and the swift, angered interjections. One man, one particular man, kept breaking in, speaking louder and louder until the passionate, furious yell of Shadrow made sense even where she stood:

"Shut your mouth!"

The bickering ceased; a long hush came. Then a man walked across the room and out of it. She heard approaching steps in the hall, a brief warning on the door. When, heart racing, she opened it, Lake Tolbert confronted her, smooth face bleaker than usual. "Your uncle," said he, "wants to see you."

She hated this man, nor could she ever meet his eyes without instinctively thinking of a reptile's blinkless, unfathomable glance. It made no difference that he presented toward her always the outer indications of courtesy, that he never failed to lift his hat or step aside at her passage; rather it only accented the feeling she had of illicit, secretive emotions burning in him. And it was odd to hear him follow her with a soft suggestion as she stepped down the hallway.

"Wouldn't allow the presence of a few men to disturb your peace of mind."

It meant nothing, yet she knew it meant something. Lake Tolbert never said an idle phrase; and so, wondering, she walked into Shadrow's office. Shadrow was there, with Maunders and three other hands. The light of bracket lamps on either wall bit into the turned faces, hardened and darkened them as they pointed at her. Tolbert quietly closed the door, stepping toward a corner. Shadrow's sagged cheeks were heavily flushed, and his narrowed eyes held a telltale gleam Lynn had come to know and to fear more than any other expression he wore.

"Lynn," he snapped, "where was you last night?"

She knew it had come. All that day the foreboding thought of it had been hanging over her head. She knew she had to lie—yet

77

to speak as much truth as she could and to lie as little as she dared. Shadrow was uncanny at catching the false note.

"Here," said she.

"All evenin'?"

"Most of it."

"Oh, so you went out? Where to?"

She watched her uncle steadily. The other men were weighing every expression on her face, judging every word she spoke. There was no friendliness in the room, no charity, no allowance for the fact that she was a woman. This was a man's ranch, and she had felt the antagonism of its members ever since her arrival on it; tonight all that antagonism seemed to burn into her. But she watched her uncle, wondering what knowledge in the hard, scheming brain of his was to trap her.

"I took the black and rode out to the south a ways."

"How far south?"

"I don't know. Two-three miles, I suppose."

"You rode out of the ranch, hey? After dark. Knowin' all the time this country is dangerous for ridin' alone?"

"Not for me," said Lynn quickly. "Why should it be?"

"You're a part of TS, ain't you?"

"No. I only live here."

"Bright answer," snorted Shadrow and pushed a pencil around the desk with his restless fingers. "You never went north, towards Hugh Tracy's?"

"No."

Shadrow leaned forward, and at sight of his face Lynn turned cold. "How was it," he demanded, "that you went away without tellin' me? And how was it you got a horse so quiet that nobody seen you go?"

"I made no particular effort to hide what I was doing," said the girl. "You men were busy with your own troubles."

Shadrow snapped out another question: "Did you keep to the road or strike across country?"

"I kept to the road, of course," said the girl, knowing that he could never check her mark of travel in all the tangle of pony tracks lying on the roadway.

"What time was it?"

"I never looked at my watch."

Shadrow said, with a deceptive unconcern: "Was it after we got through talkin' in my office?"

"I don't know," said the girl, "how long you were in your office."

Shadrow fell back against his chair with an air of being balked and turned his hard old eyes on Maunders. The gunman ripped an angry sentence at the room in general.

"Somebody's lyin'! Somebody put a bug in Tracy's ear! I rammed right into a set trap and I lost three men!"

"Well," said Shadrow, a little uncertain, "he might have been waitin' for some such play. It's natural he wouldn't sleep on the job, ain't it? Not after you boys ribbed him in Antelope."

Maunders was not to be soothed. "It won't go. When I come back I smelled dust ahead of me, all the way home. Somebody beat me to this yard just by a few minutes. I tell you, Tade, there's a nigger in the woodpile!"

All eyes turned on the girl again, raking her with a cruel suspicion. Shadrow leaned forward, returning to his harshly peremptory manner. "Lynn, you'd do a trick like that if you could. You got no love for TS. If I thought you went out there to put a bug in Tracy's ear I'd——"

Lake Tolbert cleared his throat and spoke for the first time. "She's right, Tade. I saw her get the black from the barn and mosey south on the road. Saw her come back, too. About half an hour afterwards."

Everybody in the room swung on the foreman except the girl. Shadrow's restless, calculating eyes clung to Tolbert's face a long moment. Maunders's stare freshened with bitterness.

"You was the man that told me to bust right down there and take 'em by surprise," he challenged.

"It's the way I would have done it," said Tolbert quietly.

Shadrow rapped out an irritated question: "Why didn't you speak up before, Lake?"

"She was tellin' her story," said the foreman. "I'm no hand to butt in."

"Yeah? Then why say anything now?"

"There seems to be some doubt in the room," was Tolbert's imperturbable answer.

The girl kept her face on Shadrow, not daring to look around at the foreman. The shock of his words had struck clear through her, and for a moment the room, its flittering light and its sullen occupants, became an indistinguishable blur. She knew she must have shown surprise, but the foreman's preliminary clearing of his throat had turned attention away from her; and after that she pulled herself together. Here was an ally. Yet it brought her no sense of relief. She dreaded him all the more.

"What time was all this?" grunted Shadrow.

"After I left the office," said Tolbert. "After Maunders pulled out."

Shadrow's eyes glinted; the lines of his face deepened. "Look here. You say it was half an hour before she came back. How do you know that? How could you see her come back? You was eatin' with me."

"Wasn't there more than twenty minutes," said Tolbert. "When I came out again she was just crossin' the yard from the barn."

"Something's rotten," grumbled Maunders. "And I'm the man that's going to take it in the belly. Shadrow, your damned ranch is out of kilter. Somebody's betrayin' you!"

"Me?" asked Tolbert, so toneless that Maunders hauled his big body around and let his felted wrists fall loose beside him. "Be careful what you hang on me," added Tolbert.

Shadrow's glance went prying into Tolbert's impassive face. But there was nothing to be found on that unrevealing visage, never was anything to be found on it. Shadrow rose from his chair. "Lynn, get back to your room. And don't leave this yard again unless I say so."

The girl turned, careful to avoid Tolbert's face, and opened the door in front of her. When she closed it she heard talk rise like a gust of wind. The living room was quite black, and some small squealing sliver of sound in one corner sent another current of fear through her. Hurried and full of apprehension, she went to her room.

It was Maunders who broke into angry talk after she left. "You might think everything is goin' fine, Shadrow, but it ain't! Tracy's still loose."

"He's botherin' your peace of mind?" asked Tolbert, putting an ironic slur in the words.

"There's no man that lives who bothers me!" shouted Maunders.

Tolbert showed an unusual vigor. "Then quit squawkin'. And don't lay that tongue of yours around so free."

Strained quiet came to the office. Maunders's flat features swelled with inner rage, and his nostrils flared. Yet he said nothing to the gangling foreman who confronted him with a stone-cold attention; and it was Shadrow who broke the deadlock:

"Place gettin' too small for both of you boys? Dammit, stop quarrelin'. I won't have it."

"I don't propose to be a sucker," growled Maunders.

Shadrow had a ready sarcasm for that: "Never tamper with the Lord's disposition. What's bitin' you so much? I consider we're doing well."

"Tracy loose," repeated Maunders, unable to get that out of his head. "And where's Bat Testervis? Just where is he?"

"Don't give him a second thought," said Shadrow. "He's doin' what I knew he'd do. Instead of stickin' to his quarters he's started some fool cavalry parade around the landscape. Inside of two days he won't have a dozen men left. Nobody would fight behind a plain fool like him. He's through. In the mornin' we're swingin' into his place. This plateau's mine right now—and what's the matter with that, Sid? For a big lump of nothing you show an all-fired funny streak of fidgets."

"If I don't get him, he'll get me," grumbled Maunders.

"Tracy? You bet he will." Shadrow's temper began to rise again. "I never knew a man to ruin more chances than you have, Sid. You either get him or pass out of the country. Anyhow, with the Testervis bunch gone, it's time to cut the crew. I'm payin' out too much wages. Your usefulness with me is about done, Sid. Make your play and make it in a hurry."

Unimaginative as this man was, Sid Maunders possessed some dark and obscure channels of intuition. He shook his head. "I won't be able to ride away. Tracy's a damned Indian. It's gone too far. He'd follow till I fell off the edge of creation. No, I got to cramp him some place or he'll cramp me. And, by God, Shadrow, that girl has brought nothin' but bad luck to this joint. You better do somethin' about her."

Shadrow lifted his head, lip corners full of sly malice. "I aim to."

"What's that?" broke in Tolbert.

"Marry her," said Shadrow with a tittering "he-he."

Both men showed such a plain disbelief that Shadrow slammed his hand on the table top. "You think she won't agree? By Joseph, she will—and be glad to. There's more than one way of skinnin' a cat."

Tolbert walked slowly out to the porch. In the darkness his face gave way to a wild expression of rage.

CHAPTER 9

THE UNEXPECTED

A MILE from TS, Hugh Tracy broke out of a long-maintained gallop and drifted quietly on, listening for the echo of Shadrow's outriders. Ranch lights cut a series of glowing yellow loopholes in the night, and along the windless air lay the smell of woodsmoke. Sighting nothing against the line of lights—and wondering about that—he cleared the road, curling around deep banks of shadows enfolding a string of corrals. The maneuver placed him on the east edge of the outfit and put him as well into an arroyo of some depth. Leaving the horse here, he walked back across the road. Shadrow's small saddle-stock barn laid its square pattern against the dim ranch glow; on all fours, he reached the structure and crawled as far as the plaza edge.

He knew the ranch well and could name the use of each building. Casting his glance from one point to another with a fisherman's patience, it occurred to him that the lights made a deceptive show. Very little noise came from the bunkhouses, and nobody seemed to be abroad. A calm pervaded these TS quarters, a calm arising from the semi-emptiness. Shadrow, then, had his crews out on Mogul to consolidate the victories he had won.

"He feels sure and safe," reflected Hugh.

Across the plaza on the left-hand side sat the main house with its office door wide open. Shadrow he could see rather plainly behind a desk, and he could hear other men talking. Somebody moved through the room, momentarily blanking out the light. Settling on his haunches, Tracy let the minutes ride by while he felt out the situation into which he had placed himself, calculating his own next move.

There was nothing precipitate in his advance on the TS citadel. It was not, actually, the reckless back slap he was quite capable of making. During the hot day on the ridge his thoughts had been split between his own particular problem and the extremely dangerous position of the girl. He realized that, as much as she knew of Shadrow, she didn't understand the full hazards of being in the same house with him, under his power. All his life this

82

baron had done as he willed. There never had been a bridle on his desires. Cautious and crafty and scheming—these qualities only veneered Shadrow's intrinsic ruthlessness. At heart the man was a buccaneer with a buccaneer's contempt for tribal morals. Lynn Isherwood could not know—for there was nobody in the Powder who dared tell her—of all those surreptitious stories which were household legends in the country concerning Shadrow's basic character. Whatever this man touched, ruin also touched.

So, through the grudging hours, Tracy had slowly turned this over and over in his head, increasingly oppressed by Lynn's untenable position; and he had at last come to realize that her fortune had to be his fortune. There was no way out of it. The dark weavers responsible for the affairs of humans had placed the thread of Lynn Isherwood's career across his own. The two were joined. That fact had brought him out of the ridge and placed him now beside the barn. As little as he could offer the girl in the way of security, it was better than what she had.

There was more to it, of course, than that bare and unsentimental analysis. There was a deep and stirring ferment in the very thought of this girl, and he could not shake out of his mind the picture of her—straight and inexorably honest, full of grace and vital fire. But it was like Tracy to suppress all that in his reasoning. It could have no part in the plans of a virtual bankrupt. The only thing that counted now was to get her away. And, considering his fruitless position by the plaza's edge, he realized he had to take a still more dangerous step. Coming to his knees, he rose; next moment he flattened against the barn wall.

A man came aimlessly from the direction of the main house and passed behind the barn, out of sight. A whispering undertone rose over there, and a little later Tracy saw two figures cross in front of him and head for the bunkhouse. Unknowing, they both waited out a break. Instantly accepting the chance, he slid behind the barn, paralleled it to that point where the yard narrowed into the outgoing road. The corner of the main house stood a hundred feet straight ahead, and a settling darkness hovered over everything. Walking casually into that area, he looked back at the plaza and found the two hands gone. Halfway to the house he discovered a horse standing at the porch end, and beyond that, nearer the office door, a string of six all saddled to go. Still throttling down the urge to break into a run, he swung in at the porch, stepped to it, and made the black aperture of the living-room doorway in three long strides. The house was familiar to him, and inside, edging across an absolute darkness, his stretching hands touched and identified a couch. It made a little shelter. Kneeling behind

83

it, he listened to a gusty argument boil out from the office; Maunders's voice, recognizable anywhere, grumbled along a string of words. Shadrow spoke back, swift and crackling. And he heard Lynn Isherwood's low reply.

From where he crouched he could see the suggestion of that hallway leading back from the living quarters, into which the guest rooms opened. They were all dark save one, and beneath the door of that one a penciled strip of light emerged. At the far end was another such thin glow from the kitchen. Shadrow spoke once more, answered by somebody whose tones were definite but so slurred that he could not distinguish them; immediately afterwards bodies shifted, and Tracy pulled himself below the couch a moment before the office door was thrown wide. Somebody came through, breathing fast. The door closed. Lifting his head, Hugh saw Lynn pass to the lighted bedroom and shut herself in.

What was to be done had to be done rapidly, for the conference in the office seemed to be dissolving in a quarrel. Rising from the couch, Hugh went over the living-room floor on his toes and down the hall. In front of the girl's room he drummed his fingertips softly against the panel and, without waiting for answer, pushed himself through. She came wheeling around, both hands defensively lifting. By the radiance of the half-dimmed lamp he saw that there was no color at all in her cheeks. A small gasp ran from her throat, yet as quick as he was to motion for silence she passed him, closed the door, and put her body against it.

"Hugh," she whispered, "do you know what you're doing? Oh, my dear, they would tear you apart!"

He bent near, murmuring against the shining surface of her ash-yellow hair: "You'll have to get out of here tonight."

"I can't—I don't dare—where would I go?"

"Think of that later. No time to argue about it, Lynn. If you don't slip out of here now, you never will. Understand what I mean? Now—or you never will."

She looked up, trembling; one slim hand reached out and gripped his sleeve for support. The pressure of it pulled him nearer to her almost inaudible words. "I know. But we can't! We could never get out of here! Hugh, for heaven's sake, go away!"

He shook his head. "You go down the hall first. Slip out the back livin'-room door. Wait there until——"

She let go of his arm and whirled around, both hands pressing against the door. Hugh, turned rigid, let one arm fall against his gun and remain there. Outside was the slow creep of feet. Then that sound died, and across the silence—faintly broken by the bickering from the office—a body shifted cautiously. Something scraped the wood. Looking down, Tracy saw a slip of paper appear through the bottom aperture of the door. As softly as he had come into the hallway, the unknown retreated.

Lynn swept up the paper at a single gesture and unfolded it. Watching, Hugh saw her eyes race along the writing and actually change color. She held the slip out to him. It read:

> *"Your horse was lathered last night. Don't do that again or they'll catch you."*

He looked up, puzzled. Leaning forward, she framed an almost inaudible name: "Tolbert."

The quarreling in the office had dwindled to one man's steady talk, and Hugh, astonished by the sudden swing of things, knew his tenure here was increasingly debatable. He could risk no further delay. Motioning at the door, he whispered, "Go ahead. If Tolbert's in the livin' room, speak to him so I'll know. And draw him to the back door with you. Otherwise wait out there."

She threw a strained, protesting glance at him. But he shook his head, again motioning. Stepping back, he turned the lamp wick down until a cloudy flicker of light remained. Lynn swung the door open and passed through, leaving it ajar. Hugh crossed the room and reached the hall. In this black tunnel he could see nothing at all, but he heard her moving ahead and, revolver gripped in his fist, he followed on the balls of his feet. She had stopped somewhere along the living room; and after a dragging interval, with all his nerves cold and every shred of sound magnified, he heard her expel another breath. Then he saw her cut a vague silhouette in the living-room's back doorway. Rapidly and less cautiously he went toward her.

Her throaty murmur came up beside him: "Where now? Tolbert must be around."

He caught her elbow and pulled her as far as the corner of the house, into shadows so thick as to have the motion of pooled water. From here he could command a part of the plaza, apparently empty; in any event, empty or holding men, he could no longer wait to watch. Warning her with a slight pressure on her arm, he walked straight outward from the house. Fifty yards onward he crossed the road, swerved, and went on as far as the gully. Down that a few paces he located the pony.

"Climb up."

She obeyed, but swung over, holding to him. "You are not thinking——"

"Go straight ahead at a walk, Lynn. Straight ahead till you hit the road that leads to the rim. I'll catch up."

"But you are not thinking of——"

"Lynn never mind. A gambler never looks his luck in the face. Go at a walk and keep in the road so I won't miss you."

He stepped back and waited until she had faded down the ravine, southbound. There was the small clipping echo of the pony's hoof striking some pebble, and a faint groan of leather. It was all he dared assure himself of. Turning out of the depression, he went back toward the house and gained the dark corner where he had been so shortly before. This time he skirted the side wall and came to the porch. That saddled pony on which he had pinned so much hope still stood near by. Over at the bunkhouse a hand idled in the doorway, and the argument in Shadrow's office continued on. But neither of these things bothered him so much as the threat of Lake Tolbert somewhere in the obscurity. All the rest of them might be lumped together and still fall short of the danger this one gaunt Texan contained in his single head and body. That note to Lynn, presenting a warning and a reassurance, meant nothing in the face of the foreman's record and his cold killer's instinct. If he had in any sense detected an off taint to the air this night, he would be watching. Thinking so, Hugh hooked his head around the corner and studied the porch closely. It was, so far as he could make out, clear. In the other direction—out through the throat of the yard where he must go—he could determine nothing.

Pulling himself away from the wall, Tracy walked around the end of the porch and reached the horse. He knew he had to carry it out with the lazy motions of a man doing only the natural and expected thing. The only gesture that would betray him to any covert eye in this shadow-swathed night was a motion of undue haste. Yet when he untied the racked reins and climbed into the leather there was a coat of sweat over his face, and he jammed his feet into the stirrups stiffly to keep from raking the beast out of the yard at a dead run.

The man at the bunkhouse appeared to catch the blurred shift of Tracy's body and to see in it some signal for ranch activity, for he moved into the plaza at long strides. That woke hidden figures all around the yard. A shadow detached itself from the small barn and came diagonally towards Hugh. Ten yards away, this shadow resolved to form and voice: "What's it goin' to be now?"

"Go to the office," grunted Hugh and drifted abreast the fellow.

"Who's——"

Shadrow's tones sailed out of the office into the pooled darkness. "Tolbert, I want you."

"Get over there," said Hugh to the stopped hand. And then he was past, clear of the plaza, into the road.

"Tolbert!" shouted Shadrow. "Come here!"

The poised hand shot a suddenly curious challenge at Hugh: "Who're you?"

"If you'd stuck by the barn," muttered Hugh, "instead of roamin' all around this yard, you'd know."

"Tolbert!" yelled Shadrow. "Maunders, come out here and see what the hell's goin' on yonder. Tolbert!"

Ne reply came from Tolbert—an ominous hint to Hugh. A man ran along the plaza side of the small barn and joined the inquisitive hand, who still stood uncertain in his tracks. Swift, suppressed spurts of half-angered conversation ran between them; Maunders's blundering progress came increasingly clear to Hugh, who gripped the reins with a heavy pressure. This whole situation was about to blow up violently, yet he dared not make a break for it until the two hands in his rear had lost sight of his outline and until he himself had picked up the shadow of the girl ahead. Somewhere on the dark road lay a proper deadline. Then——

He never finished the thought. There was a quick rush of a pony directly in front. A roughened voice rapped out, "Stop that! Come here, you little fool, or I'll shake the wind out of you!" Lynn Isherwood screamed, "Hugh—Hugh!" Then her appeal died abruptly and the pony drummed off into blackness. Ripping his spurs across the borrowed horse's flanks, Hugh threw himself forward. Maunders was yelling, Shadrow lifted a voice so full of rage as to sound like the screeching of a woman; and all the hands were shouting. Somebody fired a single shot. Out in front the girl cried again, and again was silenced.

CHAPTER 10

INDIFFERENT GODS LOOK ON

SLASHED by the spurs, Tracy's pony flung itself forward in great and lunging strides. Out of the ink-black foreground a solid shadow appeared, moving from left to right uncertainly, and for one wild moment Tracy thought he was lost. Bending down, he threw the whole weight of his body into an avoiding turn and, half successful, struck the shadow—Lynn Isherwood's abandoned mount—a slanting blow. His right leg scraped the beast's yielding side; stirrup and stirrup got entangled and then the free pony bucked away. The shock of that sudden strain upon the locked saddle furniture nearly unseated Tracy. All that saved him was the abrupt breaking of the empty stirrup from its holding ring. Clear then, he applied his spurs again while Lynn's horse galloped back toward TS.

The flurry checked him, put the fugitives so much farther ahead in the unseen foreground, and brought the swarming Shadrow riders so much nearer. Divided of attention, he heard Maunders's strident voice ride furiously across the night. They were in full halloo back there—all of them—and strung out along the earth. A nearer hand sent up a shouted cry: "Watch out—on the road!" A gun's echo followed closely, detonations cracking the gloom. That signal appeared to shake the TS group, to collect it, and to bring on an abrupt snarl of riders. Bedlam burst out. Distinctly he caught the dull, grunting "thwack" of a collision and its consequent cursing. One man yelled. And then there was a clear faltering of stride. Maunders was bearing away on another tangent, each pace marked by a black oath dropped; but Shadrow's half-screamed command went after the gunman imperatively and without respect or nicety. All this happened in the turn of the moments, with Tracy rushing on while a sense of needed haste prodded and nagged him. By degrees he drew clear. The sound of all that riot diminished, dwindled, and at last became only a few faint threads of murmur. The last definite thing he picked up was the backlash of a thundering quarrel between Maunders and the TS owner.

It was the first breathing spell, a respite from trouble behind. Listening now for what lay ahead, he got the rapid drumming of hoofs—of a single horse breasting the night and actually drawing away. It puzzled him, for he knew the animal to be carrying double burden—the weight of the rider and of Lynn who had been lifted from her own saddle and taken aboard the captor's. Yet the fact was so, and no more than five minutes later the last vestige of that flight fainted into the steady pound of his own pony's shoes rising rhythmically from the baked earth, to leave no guiding rumor that he might follow. As much as he wished to stop and listen, he throttled the inclination. In this touch-and-go interval he dared waste no time. So he pressed on, keeping the faintly visible strip of yellow roadway beneath him. The man ahead would, he knew, also keep to it as long as the need for fast travel was paramount.

From the moment of Lynn's warning cry, there had been no doubt in his mind as to the man's identity. All signs pointed to Tolbert. The ranch foreman's message, slipped under the door, was certainly the mark of special imterest; the foreman's disappearance from the yard, so complete that Shadrow's summons raised no answer, was a clinching of the fact. Shadrow, working out his secretive purposes within a cold and aloof brain, had at last struck. As crowded with outrage as he was, Tracy could not shake the deepening puzzlement. Abduction was a dangerous game, a reckless game—the one act certain to bring down instant pursuit. The whole county would be after Tolbert—all of Shadrow's men and some who were not. And it seemed far beside Tolbert's character thus to embark on the one act surest of evoking retaliation. The man was too canny, too certain of his ends to fly off into momentary, errant passion. What then was the answer?''

Tracy couldn't see it. Galloping along the road, he couldn't see it. All that he could make out with any degree of clarity was that he rounded into another showdown. Bill Vivian's words returned to him with an especial fitness. It was of no use to lay plans in the Powder. Nothing remained still long enough to provide any base of calculation. The only sure fact was that the dark gods attending his destiny looked on now and cared not at all. Apparently they never had. Never had any comfort come to him except by his own bitter struggle for it, and such comfort had been as transitory as the morning fog along the sand dunes. There was no end, no promise of eventual tranquillity or profit. What goodness and what order could there be in the world allowing this sequence of events to continue?

As before, there was no answer. It seemed to Tracy there never was an answer and that his life was full of dark alleys blind at the endings. Certainly nothing clear, nothing definite came of the day except only those brief moments when all the pagan splendors of the raw land stirred in him an ancient, primeval response. Such things as the crystal pathway of stars stretching across infinity, the sweep of Powder desert all golden in the morning, or some feeling of supreme fitness and unity that passed before the glow of it was quite established. Everything else was rebellion, struggle, and mischance. "Whatever I touch turns to trouble," he mused. "Whoever touches me is daubed with it."

The pony was deeply drawing, running on at a steady pace. Nothing came from the foreground. Behind, the long silence was broken by a series of out-rolling detonations that died into silence again. He had come four miles along the road, or to where it bent down into the desert via the rim's fault. Considering the route briefly, he could see no advantage in it for Tolbert. Almost certainly a TS guard stood somewhere along the fault to spot the foreman's passage and later report it to the following ranch outfit. Moreover, once the foreman reached the desert he was in a vast corral with few exits, these soon enough closed by Shadrow. In addition, Tolbert's horse could never stand the long run across the flats. It had to have a rest; and the closest hide-out would be somewhere on top of Mogul in the broken country rising sharply behind and above Antelope.

A surer test presented itself. Halted, no sound reached him. But there was a clinging dust in the air, plain indication of Tolbert's passage; and onward a hundred feet or so, where the trail forked left and right, the scent of dust bore away on the latter course into the rugged southern heights of the plateau. Tracy accepted this route and galloped half a mile before reining in, again catching the taint of the risen dust. It was as he had figured. Tolbert elected to reach quick shelter.

It was strange that the TS riders had quit, or seemed to have quit. He could make out nothing back there. For that matter, he stopped worrying about them as the packed blackness of the night increased around him and the road pitched from ravine to ridge. The dust held on, his single guide; at one point the trail crept to the very margin of Mogul's precipice, and he saw the lights of Antelope glimmer two thousand feet below. Afterwards the trail advanced boldly into the tangle of the high summits, hoisted from one increasing slope to another. The flatness of Mogul ceased to be, replaced by vague and rearing silhouettes jagged against the sky. Presently the trail lessened to a mere footway alongside the upthrust shoulders of land; a cooler, keener air washed around him, and he arrived after a while at an elevated meadow park surrounded by dense shadow. Here he stopped, defeated. The dust smell was gone.

Either he had overshot Tolbert's turn-off, or he stood now on the threshold of the foreman's new course. Whatever the case, the rocky underfooting would provide him with no more scent; nor could he hope for a sound signal, considering Tolbert's advantage of distance. That much, he reflected, was certain. It was also certain that the man's horse could not be pushed a great deal farther without rest. It thus became an even bet that Tolbert would accept the first good hide-out he reached.

There, in the dark, Tracy blocked out the surrounding country in his mind. Obviously the man was running south—the one sure way of getting out of the Powder. Still, in the south stood a stiff and immediate climb that would be difficult for a jaded beast, while onward a mile there was another trail leading in the desired direction by gentler grades. And off there lay a hundred by-passes Tolbert might take, each adjacent to isolated ravines and commanding viewpoints such as a fugitive might well use to survey the back trail when light came. More important, in that region were three line cabins.

Tracy went slowly forward. A small breeze scoured the slopes, setting up thin waterfalls of sound; and the click of the pony's shoes made little javelin echoes. It was a dull and straining business to cruise at this speed. As so many times before, there was a violent discord in him between the patience he never sufficiently possessed and his natural desire to break forward impetuously. What held him was a clear and increasing realization of Lake Tolbert's essential power. The man knew all the tricks and would use them. He was, Tracy summed up, an Apache in temperament.

Somewhere beyond, Tracy angled up the slope of a small ridge, cut across its spine, and dismounted, to descend the other side a good hundred yards before halting. Here he crouched, seeing nothing in the dense blackness below, but knowing a deserted cabin to be there. Listening with a collected and profound attention, he wondered again what Tolbert could hope for, what remote advantage he could be foreseeing. There was no answer save one—and that too brutal to be probable. Nothing moved yonder—the cabin was empty. Swinging back to the horse, he sidled into a gulch, rode it out, and thereafter tackled the stiffly pitched slopes. It was a blind man's game, to be played against one who never would allow himself the error of underestimating pursuit. Long afterwards Tracy came to another hidden hollow and again repeated his silent skirting of a log hut invisible in the depths. As before, the guess was wrong; and as before, he pressed on.

Threading the black defiles, he lost all sense of time. It might have been an hour or it might have been four hours since he had left TS. His only gauge of the night was the varying thickness of fog layers as he rode through them. Around what he believed to be midnight he finally came out upon a dominating peak of the Moguls and stopped to consider. Any way from this point he might command a view of the hills when day arrived; and as much as he despised the logic of the thought, it seemed best to wait out the day. Further groping was entirely futile. Tolbert was halted—that he knew; and halted within striking distance of this peak.

"I'll learn a little patience before I die," grunted Tracy, and unsaddled in a slight bowl below the cone of the peak. Rolling in the blanket, he fell into an intermittent sleeping and rousing. From another angle of the dark world came the abysmally melancholy wail of a coyote.

What woke him, just when the first pale wedge of light broke the eastern black, was the faintest reverberation of sound passing along the utter quiet of the morning. Rising instantly, he made his way to the top parapet of rock and stationed himself behind it. In every direction, at this hour, he viewed only low-lying layers of fog banked in the depressions like deep drifts of snow. Gradually, as the glow strengthened out of the east, the top mists broke, and one after another the higher promontories pierced the thinning blankets; then all at once the fog in the ravines began to eddy and run as water might, exposing the whole southern distance in its gaunt and broken outline. Yonder a mile, he sighted one of the cabins he had in mind and, looking at it with a concentrated attention, he thought he made out the shift of a body in the doorway. It was a slim enough chance, yet he moved directly back to the horse. He saddled and led it down the blind side of the peak a full three hundred yards before mounting; then he cut a circle across the lower ground and struck into a gulch. It lead south. It brought him by changing degrees around the peak. It went descendingly on, side walls effectually hiding him. Keeping the peak's spire as a compass point, Tracy arrived at timber and here rose from the gulch to begin another curling foray. Night damp was on the ground, and the green pine needles glistened in the fresh and sunless light. One faint shred of activity twined through the trees. Stopped dead, he jumped from the horse, crawled up an incline, and found himself staring at the back side of the cabin through a narrow aperture in the timber mass. He had made a complete half-circle from the back of the peak.

The cabin was two hundred feet forward and without a window on this side. A saddled horse stood there grazing. Alert now and expecting anything, Tracy flattened against the earth mold and placed one quick glance after another long the vistas presented to him. Tolbert was not to be caught thus easily off balance, and the very air of quiet held a warming. Yet his free running inspection could locate no direct evidence of such; and urged on by a lack of faith in his position, he crawled through the pines, a yard at a time, until he reached a place abreast the cabin's front and perhaps sixty feet away from it. From this point clear ground swept onward to the peak. Lynn Isherwood sat on a log by the doorway with her face lifted to that commanding summit.

He saw her profile to be clear and calm, almost without strain, and instantly one great fear left him. She was exactly as she had been at TS the previous night—ash hair smoothed back from her temples, rough gray shirt open at the throat. All her body was in repose, and her hands were quiet in her lap; she had courage—that fine quality of courage which was steady and dominating and never needed the false stimulant of anger to buoy it up. A moment later her head came around to reveal the long shadows across those gray-blue eyes. Puzzlement made quick, deep creases on her brow.

Tracy went rigid in his place, and his breathing turned small and slow. There was no sound inside the cabin, no trace of Tolbert. The man was outside somewhere, hidden and hunting; venturing a slight sidewise roll, he searched the roundabout trees with a roused sense of catastrophe. He had gained this shelter too easily. Tolbert had let him pocket himself. Thinking so, he was on the verge of crawling to better shelter when he saw Lynn rise from the log and turn slowly away. That and the rustling of brush on the far side of the cabin arrested him, made him reach for the holstered gun. A man called and came out of the trees on a trot, smiling; and at sight of him Tracy was astonished out of all his set convictions. For that figure stepping into the clear and facing Lynn with a half-hunted, half-sardonic expression on his ruddy cheeks was not Tolbert. It was Bat Testervis—Bat Testervis unshaven and unhandsome.

Testervis spoke to the girl with a quick, overbearing insolence. "You had a chance to make a run for it. Why didn't you try?"

She said nothing, and he fell to impatient anger. "I'm getting pretty sick of this freeze-out manner. Look here, Lynn, I'll break that unnecessary pride or I'll break your neck."

"I can't follow all your quick changes," said she calmly. "First you'll sweep up the earth for me, then you'll break my neck. What can I depend on, Mr. Testervis?"

"Be reasonable," said Bat, of a sudden persuasive.

"Are you?"

Testervis shrugged his wide shoulders. "You told me once I didn't have nerve. I figured maybe that was why you never liked me. Well, I set out to show you I had it. Did, didn't I? I took you right out from under Tade Shadrow's nose."

"What for?" challenged the girl. "Are you big enough fool to think I can be persuaded that way?"

"If," argued Bat, wholly in earnest, "you saw me as I really was—not as you've made up your mind I must be—you wouldn't be as chilly. What's a woman want if not a man that can take care of her?"

"And you thought I might be made to like you by force?" retorted the girl.

There was a biting irony in it, but Testervis, normally thin-skinned enough to feel the faintest hint of affront, seemed not to be aware of it now. He was involved in his own thought endeavoring to get it across. "Never mind how I did it, Lynn. There wasn't any other way left open to me. My outfit is through—all gone. I figured I might hit back, but the crew left me flat. I'll never ride this country any more. All I can do is run. What else could I do but watch my chance to catch you alone?"

"What for?" challenged the girl, insistently abrupt.

"Why," said the man, very slowly choosing his words, "I've told you already. You had the wrong idea of me. I knew if I could get you on even ground it would be different. Forget what Tade's told you. Forget what anybody's told you about Bat Testervis. I'm no wolf. I'm a human bein'. I can make my way anywhere. I'm not afraid of anything that breathes."

"What for?" repeated Lynn Isherwood.

Testervis stared, the ruddy complexion taking on a deeper flush. "I want an even chance—same as you'd give any man you met for the first time. Drop all the nonsense that's been loaded onto you."

"You're a fool," stated the girl. "An arrogant, bumptious fool. What you really had in your mind was that no woman could possibly resist your charm once she saw it. Well, you've made the best of the chance you had—and it hasn't worked. I'm

94

sorry, but I don't see you. My first impression was right. You haven't succeeded in changing it. You strut and you brag. Down in your heart you're a bully—otherwise you wouldn't be thinking plain strength pleased any woman who had sense.''

"Wait a minute," said Bat, a sullen anger showing out of his big eyes. "Don't get me wrong again. I had no wild ideas about abductin' you at all. I made that play to show I wasn't afraid of TS. Also to have a few uninterrupted hours to explain myself—which you always refused to let me have.''

"All right. I'll agree you've proved your great courage.''

Tracy's admiration for the girl deepened enormously. She was jabbing Bat's pride, rubbing salt into his egotism with a wicked deliberation, surely knowing the danger she thereby ran. Bat Testervis visibly swelled with rage, and thick color ran solidly up his columnar neck. The cigarette in his hand shook; and the staring surfaces of his eyes assumed a sultry glare visible even across the distance. When he spoke again, Tracy heard the man's temper beat harder against the restraining calm.

"After I'd made that clear, I never had the least intention of carrying you farther off—unless you wished to go. I meant to let you do as you pleased. That was the extent of it. I'm not crazy. I know what comes to a man that tries a kidnappin stunt. It would be playin' right into Tade Shadrow's hands. So I figured to let you go, or to help you get out of the country if you wished.''

"I'll settle your doubt," said Lynn coolly. "Leave me right here.''

"You'll never get the chance to decide now!" cried Testervis, all at once overwhelmed by madness. "I have changed my mind! You'll string along with me till I get some humbleness into your system!''

"Better let me go now," answered Lynn, unshaken. "You know what will happen to you if you're caught.''

"I don't propose to be caught! By God, I hope Shadrow and his pack keep comin'! I'll do some long-distance damage on my own account for what they've done to me! As for you and your fine airs, you'll sure start regrettin' all that sarcasm and contempt you've laid onto me!''

"And now you're mad," said Lynn Isherwood.

"You're worth kissin'," muttered Testervis and suddenly walked toward her. Lynn's hand struck him so sharply across the face that the report was like a muffled gunshot. Testervis seized the arm before it fell and twisted it toward him. Then he let it drop, staggering back, sullen emotions congealing on his cheeks. Hugh

Tracy stood upright in the clearing, cold and soundless, revolver pinned on the other's broad chest.

"Step aside, Lynn," said Tracy in the flattest speech a man could ever make. The girl, startled, wheeled about with a breath rushing through her throat. As soon as she saw him, saw the incredible fire of his eyes, she cried out:

"No—Hugh—no!"

"Lynn," droned Hugh Tracy, "he's dirt beneath your feet. You ought to realize it by now. Step aside."

"Don't do it—don't do it, Hugh!"

"He was a spoiled and coddled kid," said Hugh, unrelentingly stolid. "He never knew how to lose his marbles without cryin'. He was a tricky, mean, short-tailed little rat. And he grew up worse. As long as he gets his own way, he's a lion. When the goin' turns a little tough, he's a yellow-bellied squealer."

"Don't," repeated Lynn Isherwood rapidly. "Never mind what he is. You can't afford to be cruel, Hugh!"

"I told you," grunted Hugh, "I didn't believe in Santy Claus."

Testervis stood dumb, flat in his tracks, motionless since that first surprise of Tracy's appearance. His breathing came labored and fast. Both big fists hung to his hip line; and either through fear or that madness which destroys, the ruddiness of his skin vanished entirely, to leave a strained white mask in which the two bold eyes gleamed with utter malevolence. He had his head back, and those eyes, winkless, never left Hugh Tracy's gripping inspection.

"He's lost," said Lynn Isherwood. "Isn't that enough, Hugh?"

"Not for me. All his miserable life he's got out of scrapes without payin'. This time he's got to take his medicine. Turn around, Bat."

Into the other man's congested, hating glance appeared a distinct break of alarm. "You're not goin' to——"

"If I was able to shoot you from behind I would," said Hugh. "But it ain't in me. Turn around. Lift your hands high."

Testervis swung reluctantly, obeying. Hugh walked forward and reached out to get the man's gun from its holster, and to throw it far into the trees. He retreated then and dropped his own gun to the earth. "All right," said he. "Come on at me."

Testervis wheeled, fury exploding. He yelled savagely. "You sucker, that's what I hoped you'd do! I'll bust your back in the middle!" Lynn Isherwood, half swinging toward him, cried out. But Testervis suddenly grinned in a manner that pulled his lips apart, drew himself to his full height and leaped forward.

Against that swelling spread of shoulder and that thickness of torso, Hugh Tracy's own rugged body seemed slender and ineffectual by comparison—without a chance of stopping the rushing attack. For Testervis came on as if the savage momentum of his heavy body would beat Hugh Tracy to earth and leave him there senseless; his blond head, lowered like a battering ram, shone in the first morning sun, and he emitted a strangled cry that blasted the still air as his two club-like arms stretched outward. Hugh, cold and clear of mind, took a single pace to the rear, balanced himself, and shot ahead. Between those destructive arms was an opening into which he drove a sledging blow, straight for the pit of Bat's stomach. The wind spilled out of Testervis. He lost control of his assaulting bulk and hit Hugh as so much dead weight, the point of a shoulder crushing Hugh's chest. Yet, even bereft of the full driving power, it was a numbing impact and Hugh went staggering away from it, shivered to the bone. Bat's face lifted in contorted satisfaction; he sucked in air with a retching effort, and he lunged on once more to land a blow against Hugh's temple. Hugh, all the world gone black, ran in and gripped the big fellow desperately about the chest. He could see nothing, hear nothing. Bat's hot breath burned his neck, and he felt himself being lifted and whirled and shaken ferociously while something kept grinding on his instep and hammering at his groin. Yet he hung on for what seemed an interminable length of time, and was dimly surprised when the dense mists cleared and he found himself still weathering through, still pinning Bat's arms. The big man was vomiting out his rage, making great and staggering lunges across the dirt with this leech-like burden.

Hugh let go abruptly and struck for the broad shelving of Bat's chin—a direct exploding hit that sent the man back on his heels. It threw Bat off guard as well, spread his arms apart, unbalanced him for a moment; and in that moment Hugh smashed the bold face left and right and stood idle while Testervis went spinning to earth. Sweat streamed down Hugh's jaw and worked like fire on a bruise made by some blow he didn't remember. He was reaching deeply for wind, starved for it, unable to get enough, and all the while standing over Testervis, who lifted himself on one elbow and glared out of eyes gone pale violet.

"You're not through!" cried Testervis. "You'll fight till your damned heart breaks! I'll smash you to pulp!"

"Come on—come on up," said Tracy.

Testervis rolled away, got on all fours, crouching. He flashed a glance slyly back; he sprang up and away like a runner, and wheeled instantly afterwards, defenses risen. But Hugh Tracy, the rank taste of blood in his mouth, was ridden relentlessly by the black, smoldering lust to destroy. Whatever he normally was, mercy was out of him now and all sense of pain or danger or caution. He threw himself at the swinging Testervis and was checked by stiff-armed jabs that went wild and sank into his neck and chest. He never felt them. His own blows beat down those barrier-like assaults until Bat's face was a clear target in front of him, round and swollen and white. He smashed it, he ripped it side to side; he flung one blasting jab after another at it until he saw nothing there. And when the tempest cleared from his brain, he looked down and saw Testervis silent on the ground. The big prone shoulders shook as if Testervis were crying.

"Get up and come at me," said Tracy.

Testervis slowly put his hands beneath him and fell back.

"Get up," snapped Tracy. "You're not through."

But Testervis rolled his head from side to side on the earth and brought his palms up to cover it as might a sick man shutting out the world. Hugh Tracy stared, speechless. The livid temper subsided, and the bruises on his own body began to throb. He was finished. The fury that had carried him so far went away— and left him filled with disgust, as always. Turning toward the girl standing by the cabin, he spoke slowly:

"I'm sorry you had to see it. You've seen me as Powder sees me—and it is not a pretty sight. I'm no better a savage than they say."

She watched him, wide-eyed, whispering; "Nothing—nothing could stand against you, Hugh. Not when you're roused."

"Bat," grunted Hugh, "you're licked all ways. Best you can do now is get up and travel till the sun finds you in another country. I'm keepin' your horse for Lynn. I'm keepin' your gun. If I gave it to you, you'd shoot me in the back—and I don't blame you for wantin' to do it. Get up and go."

Testervis reared back on his knees, shaking his head stupidly. He got to his feet and pressed his fingers across his eyes. When he cleared them and looked at Tracy once more, they were blank of feeling.

"You're settin' me afoot and harmless—in the Powder? Look here, Tracy, Shadrow's got me marked."

"Then stay out of sight and travel by dark," returned Tracy.

"I may get clear at that," said Testervis, displaying no heat. "But you and the girl won't. They'll hound you and they'll catch you. I only wish I could be around to see them do it. It's me that put them on the scent, and it's you they'll find. I've been sick of this mighty-man-Tracy stuff for years. Wherever I went I bumped

98

into it. Well, let's see the mighty man get clear of this. You're finished."

"Travel," ordered Tracy. "You never did learn to lose without cryin'."

"You're finished!" cried out Testervis wildly, and started off. Standing in his tracks, Tracy watched the man go limping across the flat ground and up the side of the ridge. He disappeared in timber and came to view once more on the ridge's crest; then, without looking back, he passed down the other side.

"I'm sorry for him," said Hugh.

Lynn Isherwood lifted her chin, shadows disappearing from her face. Quick pleasure appeared there on the clear, steady features. "I knew you'd say that, Hugh."

"He's got a long course to the south," mused Tracy. "But he loves his skin and he'll make it."

He was mistaken in Testervis. Well as he knew the man, he had no conception of the subterranean fires that worked through Bat. Once over the hill, Testervis turned north, back around the peak, instead of south. He traveled steadily up the long grade and out to a slight promontory from which he could view part of that broken land falling into TS range; and pausing there, he saw a single rider curling around the trail something more than a mile distant. Thoughtful and taciturn, he stood still a long interval, then at last went ahead, fashioning his own route to fall eventually into that trail. The rider came steadily on, growing to definite shape in the saddle—long-legged, abnormally tall of upper parts, and strangely immobile. It was, Testervis presently saw, Lake Tolbert. Testervis came to a full stop and let his hand drop to the empty holster. Swearing softly, he scanned the farther landscape for men to follow up the TS foreman. But there were none in view.

"Always one trick left in the deck," he muttered, and held his ground.

Tolbert, he realized, must have identified him before now. But the foreman neither checked in nor displayed any particular sign of increased wariness. Sure and unbending, he arrived at within ten yards before he halted and stared at the battered figure blocking the trail.

"A surprise to you?" asked Testervis.

"Nothin' ever surprises me," said the foreman laconically. "Where's the girl?"

"How do you know——"

"I know," said Tolbert.

99

"Well, I'm through," muttered Testervis. "I'm licked and I realize it. But I've got a dicker to make with Shadrow."

"Dicker?"

"He wants the girl, don't he? He wants Tracy?"

Tolbert's narrowed eyes remained inscrutably on the man. "How is it," he mused, "that a Testervis would come about like this?"

"That's my business," retorted Bat. "But if I'm licked, I'm licked. Willing to admit it. Shadrow will find his hand considerably strengthened by a little legality in this mess. I'll sign over the ranch for any sort of figure, and I'll do him some good to boot. More's the point right now, I can take him direct to Hugh Tracy."

"Seems odd," reflected Tolbert with a faint singsong in the words.

Testervis moved uneasily. "Never mind. You're no hand to inquire into a man's reasons."

"Not inquirin'," said Tolbert. "Already know."

"You don't know a damned thing," snapped Testervis.

"Where are they?"

"Behind me, not far off. Is Shadrow around?"

Tolbert elected to say nothing, but Testervis found his answer in the lower distance. Over on the flats of the Mogul a long gray column advanced beneath a rolling cloud of dust. Seeing that, something happened to the man's face. Distinctly it sharpened with excitement and uncertainty. Tolbert's seizing glance absorbed the fact. Shifting in the saddle, he spoke with the same colorless inflection:

"Wouldn't be too sure of Tade's friendliness. Keep away from him. Leave the country. Don't you know what sort of a reception you'll get from the man?"

"I ain't worryin'," countered Bat, irritably. "So why should you?"

"Friendly suggestion."

"Friendly hell!"

"Tracy ran into you," reflected Tolbert. "And like to addled your brains. That's why you're sellin' out."

Testervis glared at the motionless man above him, big eyes suffusing with anger. Tolbert went on, relentless.

"And took your gun and told you to scatter. To get even with him, you'd risk your neck. You'd traffic with the outfit that killed your brother and ruined your own fortune. It's more than odd, Testervis. It's a weasely shift. Some things, friend, no man can afford to do."

"Why, you damn scoundrel!" yelled Testervis. "What kind of a fellow are you to preach at me?"

Tolbert's gimlet eyes bored into the other, and the flat words fell one by one: "Supposin' that girl might want to get away from TS? Make any difference in your style?"

"She had a chance with me," muttered Testervis. "She turned it down. Why should I care what happens to her?"

Tolbert was silent, turning back for a short look at the cavalcade swinging up through the lower draws. Again facing Testervis, he said: "Better not try it. Tade's won his battle and he'll need no help from you. You're liable to get in a jam."

"I'll see Shadrow about that," growled Testervis.

"Nothing will change your mind?"

"I'll see Shadrow," insisted Testervis. "Look here, I don't savvy what you're trying to do. You work for TS, don't you?"

"I see," said Tolbert. "Nothing will change your mind." The stiffness of his body increased, and the thin mouth became bloodless. "Some things, Testervis, are plumb unnatural in a man. Even in a weak and bad one. You fool." The long arm whipped down against the blackened gun butt exposed. Testervis cried out his alarm.

"Tolbert——!"

There was one sharp and rolling explosion. The snout of the gun kicked in Tolbert's fist. Bat Testervis, horrified astonishment on his cheeks, pitched to the earth and died face down.

"Never had a lick of sense in him," said Tolbert. For one considerable interval he stared at the ground, little eyes guiltless of any feeling, rigidly controlled by the aloofness always abiding with him. Afterwards he holstered his piece and turned around. Looping along the mountain side, he met the cavalcade some twenty minutes later on a lower level. Shadrow was leading.

"What was that shot?" asked the TS boss.

Tolbert silently pointed in the general direction of southeast—a good forty-five degrees aside from that peak behind which Tracy and the girl were hidden. Then, when Shadrow's inspection grew insistent, the foreman said laconically: "I saw nothing over toward the west. We better follow that echo."

"Seemed to come more out of the due south to me," objected Shadrow.

"I was nearest it," replied Tolbert impatiently.

"Go ahead, then. Aim for it."

Accepting the lead, Tolbert led the party on into the deeper ruggedness of Mogul, but wide of the peak.

CHAPTER 11

FLIGHT

HUGH TRACY watched Testervis until the latter disappeared from the ridge. Then he swung abruptly on the girl. "Lynn——"

She interrupted him. "No. Nothing happened." A fine color crept across her cheeks, but her eyes clung to him without embarrassment. "You are a direct man, Hugh."

"I know Bat," said Tracy. "Sooner or later he'd crossed the line."

She nodded slowly. "I realized that."

"Where," darwled Hugh, "did you learn to be so cool under fire?"

"I grew up amongst all kinds of men, Hugh. My father ran a ferry, a hotel, and a saloon. I could swear before I could read."

"I'm glad I'm here," he grumbled.

"My dear man," said the girl with a gentle gayety, "you don't know how glad I am."

"Now we've got to dust along."

"Hugh, I'm not so sure about that."

He shook his head. "Shadrow and his boys will be somewhere right over that peak. This is broken country and good shelter, but it is dangerous to be in. If he works it right he can bottle us up. Sooner we're out of it, the better."

She was watching the first broad yellow bands of sunlight break across the peak's sharp tip. A frown lay lightly penciled on her forehead, and her lips were thoughtfully pursed. Yet somehow this show of concern had little effect on the resiliency and freshness of spirit showing through the expressive features. Even now he caught the hint of slight recklessness, of a gambling instinct; this and a serene poise hard to shake. "Wait a minute, Hugh. What Bat Testervis said was really true. He brought my uncle on the trail. And you'll be the one to suffer for it. If it is as risky as you say, I'd better ride back while you ride on."

"What in thunder do you suppose I came to TS last night for?"

"I know. But isn't there always another day and another

chance? I can't allow the thought of you being caught by Tade. I know even better than you do what would happen."

"Further, deponent sayeth not," drawled Hugh. "You have spoken your piece. Now we'll get out of here."

The lurking smile broke through. "At least I had the chance to say what I should say, Hugh. Now I'll say no more. You don't realize how wonderful it is to put the burden on your shoulders." The smile disappeared before a deep, deep gravity. "You don't really know. I ought to despise myself for being so wishy-washy."

"I guess I can take the burden with no great hurt," said Hugh, equably.

"That's just the trouble," she retorted. "Don't you suppose I have heard enough about you to draw my own conclusions? Actually, you have been so willing to assume other people's burdens that they impose on you. That's how you've gotten such a reputation for fighting. You'd take my troubles to yourself if they broke your back. Hugh, my idea is really best."

"Return to Tade?" grunted Tracy. "Some day let me tell you about that relation of yours. There is no going back now. Wait here."

"It is a very faint and very distant relationship," said the girl. "His branch of the family is so far from mine that he's actually not a true uncle."

He went around the house, got his horse and led it by Bat's tethered mount. When he brought them both into the clearing, the girl was coming out of the cabin with her coat. "Which way, Hugh?"

"South—due south." He held his own horse while she stepped into the saddle.

"Where does it lead?"

"Out of Powder," said Hugh, mounting and swinging about. "Out of the country just as far as we can get out."

"And then where?" murmured the girl, more to herself than to him. Of a sudden the cloud was across her eyes again.

"Time enough to consider it when we are clear," answered Hugh. "First things first."

"First things first," repeated the girl. "Yes—that would be your way. It is strange. I have heard so much of you that I can almost tell what you'll do when something comes up—tell it before you act. You believe in having a hard chore over with, don't you?"

"If I stopped to do any serious thinking," said Tracy, "I'd be in bad shape. Some men get fat on study. All I get out of it is a feeling that there ain't anything worth fighting for. So I quit studyin'."

"There's a reason for that, too," mused the girl.

"What's the reason?"

She shook her head. "Not now, Hugh. But you wouldn't be running, would you, if I hadn't gotten in your road? No, I'm pretty sure of it. You'd be circling the edges, waiting to hit back."

"Presently occupied doing just that," said Tracy.

"See what trouble a woman can make?" Lynn murmured. "Yet all I can say is that I am in your hands—and glad of it."

"Forward."

Out of the distance lifted the thin echo of a shot. Only one, fading down the sides of the peak. It brought the startled look back into the girl's eyes, but Hugh, alert, nodded his head slowly. "That places part of the bunch. Right behind us. Here we go, Lynn."

He led through the pines and into a small ravine. Abreast, they went along this at a trot, feeling the freshness of the morning slowly evaporate into the strengthening heat. Ahead lay the banked ridges, each feeding into the other and all timbered. It was a secretive land, alike protective and deceptive; for it offered the searching TS crew the same shelter it offered him. Now regarding his surrounding quarters with a roving eye, he pulled out of the ravine, passed across a small bare knob, and plunged into timber again. A thin, sunless trail led upward by looping stages. It was single file once more, the girl silent behind.

Going along with his attention fixed outward, he reflected that this girl whose perceptions were so direct and to the point had laid the situation clear enough; but for her presence in his affairs he would not now be pointed southward out of the fight. In effect, he was running away—and would continue to run as long as she had need of him. It was puzzling to understand by just what joining of events and at just what stage of time Lynn's life had come so definitely between him and his business. But it was so—the shift had been made. Now that he gave it more than a moment's consideration, it astonished him enormously to note how casual and inevitable was the complete change of weight from his own fortunes to the girl's. He who always clung to the main issue through principle was far afield. In a degree this retreat meant a collapse of his resistance, for his luck depended entirely on staying within striking distance of Shadrow and waiting for a break. This was the only kind of a fight he could wage; and he was too old a hand in trouble not to understand that once he ceased to hit back he was through. Some sort of queer destiny arranged these things. No man's luck held when the chances went cold. He had staged one return; he could not successfully stage another. Next time Powder country would be closed to him. The struggle over, Shadrow would arrange all the safeguards and barriers.

Yet with this fact definitely established, Hugh Tracy felt neither regret nor resentment. The aimless wheel of chance had pitched him into this—that was the sum of it. He knew that he would go on with the girl, see her to safety. First things first. Turning, he found her eyes fixed on him with an oddly level, steady light. When he resumed his frontwise survey it was to feel a sweeping access of energy and anger.

Her voice came ahead with a small musical lift. "Was that scowl for me or for the universe, Hugh?"

"Was I?"

"Didn't know you were? That means some long-range thinking. What about, Hugh?"

"Better not say."

"Good or bad thoughts?"

"Sort of like a mirage—mighty nice but not permanent."

There was no answer for a long while. But, deeper in the shaded silence, she said wistfully: "Usually some foundation for a mirage, Hugh. That water floating in the sky comes from a river somewhere actually running."

"Too far off for a thirsty fellow."

"Hugh," she said, peremptorily, "there's a streak of unhappiness in you. Why?"

It was some little time before he answered that, and then very slowly. "I should like to believe in many good things and can't see my way clear to do it. Ever notice a horse barred from a green field, looking at it with his under lip drooping?"

"You've had to fight fire with fire too long," said the girl thoughtfully. "And I wonder it hasn't made you more bitter than you are. Listen, Hugh, if you believe in the Powder philosophy of strong hand winning, and if there is something you want real bad, why don't you reach out and take it?"

"Things worth having don't come that way," replied Hugh promptly.

"Then," said Lynn, voice quickening, "you are not the savage you think you are."

"Which leaves us right where we started."

"No," said the girl, "it doesn't."

"About this being a savage. What if I were?"

Lynn Isherwood said quietly, "It would make no difference—to me."

"Wait here."

The trail pitched up to a square clearing not more than an acre in extent. Halted on the margin of it, Tracy studied its edges cautiously, glance digging into the farther alleyways of pine. After a moment he went across it, saw nothing, and motioned for the girl to come along. She arrived on the gallop, and at this pace they pressed forward, still higher and still sheltered. It was soft underfoot, but now and then one of the drooping hoofs struck rock, and the muted echo of it rose accented in the pervading hush of this isolated country. By degrees the trail fell off from the south to the southwest; and ahead of them, masked by the timber but nevertheless indicated by the contour of the earth, was the beginning of a pass that struck directly into the up-thrust terrain. By ten o'clock they had arrived in the heaviest of the Mogul country; at noon, going at no more than a walk, they came to the lower stages of the pass. Tracy turned off and led the way up a stringer of land that ended in a shelf. The district through which they had traveled all that morning ran away below them, gulch crisscrossing gulch. Out of the depths came a swift and passing beam of light. Instantly Tracy focused his attention on the spot.

"Sun hit some bright metal," he muttered. "Now look yonder at that little meadow."

She saw them, following his outstretched arm; a column of them, single-file, going without haste over the open. "Hugh," she said, "it doesn't look to be such a big party."

"That's the trouble," answered Tracy. "Tade's split his men. He knows he's on the right track, and he suspects what I'm aiming to do. Unless I'm wide of the mark, he's figuring to get around us."

Meanwhile his running glance passed slowly off to the westward—to the heaving summits in the yonder distance. Here and there some small burn or park broke the spired ranks of pine. Far away a bare ridge creased the emerald green. Along these breaks Tracy kept his attention, looking at one and the other.

"What does Tade think you're going to do, Hugh?"

"Cross over the summit to the west and fade into that country," replied the man, eyes narrowed against the down-plunging sun shafts. "Over there the timber runs on for better than fifty miles, clear to the state line. If we make it, we're out of the Powder complete and Tade can't afford to follow. We're clear. Otherwise——"

106

"Otherwise we're going to run into something different on to the south?"

Suddenly he lifted his long arm to the west. "Away ahead. Above this snag. Follow past it to that patch of yellow you can just see."

But she shook her head after a prolonged inspection. "Don't see anything."

"Nevertheless, there's a party filing into Fremont Basin, which is where this pass lets out. If we tackled the pass we'd run right into them."

"You've got the eyes of an eagle."

Tracy turned downgrade, the girl falling behind; and the man chuckled a little as he talked over his shoulder. "If it's a compliment, Lynn, you better use a different bird. It's the turkey vulture that sees well. He can leave an eagle flat-footed on the perch. Well, we've got to continue due south, which is not so good."

"Why?"

"There's a stretch of open flat desert away ahead of us. If we can't cross this peak country and go west, we'll have to cross the desert. That's what Tade is working for right now."

The girl was silent, and Hugh looked around, shaking his head. "Now I shouldn't have said anything about it."

"I am in your hands," smiled the girl. "And glad of it."

A long riding silence fell between them as they traveled through the afternoon, on and on into the sustained quiet of the trees. All that broke it was the slow stamp of hoofs, the slight squeak of leather, and the little jingle of bridle chains. Once, around what might have been two o'clock, they arrived at a bubbling spring and stopped for a drink; and for a few short minutes they rested, wordless. Afterwards resuming the flight, Tracy left what seemed the fairest trail and began a venture along one half-obliterated runway and another. The throat of the pass was high-water mark for them, and now they were tending steadily downward, into the heavier heat that cushioned the rugged earth; by degrees the underbrush lessened and they passed into an unending prospect of senna-red pine trunks shooting up from a thick carpet of forest mold, which received and made soundless the pacing of the horses.

Any other day this virgin wilderness would have been splendid adventure. But the girl, watching Tracy's head swing from side to side with an increased vigilance and seeing his face more deeply trenched by his characteristic half-scowl, was stirred with the imparted feeling of approaching danger. The very quiet bred it. Drawn into herself, and not wishing to disturb him, she tried to fathom his strategy from watching their course. And finally she understood the meaning of the apparent zigzag advance. Along a vista she viewed the up-slanting sides of a butte. Tracy motioned her to stay in place and spurred forward to quick slopes that achieved a bare and broken top partially in sight. Leaving the saddle, she rested on the earth, grateful for the chance. Time dragged out, and the persistent hush actually oppressed her to the point where she began studying the corridors of this forest for hostile life. The curt, low call of a bobwhite startled her as the boom of a cannon might have done.

Tracy came back a good quarter-hour later, fine sweat cropping out on his forehead and heavy angles around the lip corners. "Onward, Christian soldiers. By any chance do you happen to miss breakfast and dinner?"

"Hadn't given them a thought," lied Lynn.

"Good girl, it's a long time between drinks and we're going to move a little faster."

"Trouble in sight?"

"Nothing to speak of," said Hugh.

But she was not deceived, for when they got into motion again she saw the direction change. Hugh veered off from the east and pointed directly south once more. Passing by the butte, they went between the walls of a rocky gulch and on into a changed terrain. Nothing could have been more abrupt than this remarkable transformation from the comparatively undulating belt of pines to the jagged and grotesque area ahead. It was such a country to which the West often applies the label "devil's garden" with ample fitness. There was no apparent open trail through this maze of strewn slabs and great barriers of basaltic rock cliffs lifting from thirty to a hundred feet above them. One narrow chasm after another marched to an obvious blind end; yet at each such end Tracy always swung into some sort of avenue or tunnel that led forward. Hot sunlight passed overhead; half-twilight remained below. Stunted jack pines clung to these sharp slopes with a dogged tenacity. And it was cool here, cool with the promise of hidden water.

In spite of the tortuous route, Tracy kept the ponies at a trot, charging down the straightaways, idling around the bends until Lynn's head grew dizzy with the constant strain of anticipated trouble; and so wrapped up in it was she that sundown came unawares and dusk followed the blue-shot summer's twilight. Tracy left her again to climb a more accessible promontory.

After a while he returned, his body only a faint silhouette above the horse.

"Tired?"

"No," said Lynn.

"You're not deceiving me any," said Tracy gently. "But we'll have to go on for a while yet. Follow me a little closer. We're soon out of this gorge—and into another one."

Full dark dropped without warning, and there was only a faint strip of starlight above—a crooked strip cut out by the narrow gorge rims. For a space she tried to rein the pony after Tracy, but it only seemed to make the animal stumble, so she gave up the attempt and let it have free head. Weariness arrived soon enough, leaving her spine numb and her arms heavy. Once she thought she slept, for Tracy's words came to her with a sort of continued effect, as if he had been speaking before. They reached an open area where the color of the night turned gray and a piece of wind struck them slantwise. But it was of short duration, and afterwards they appeared to descend into still greater depths of this tortured land. A rolling, spraying sound came from ahead, and Tracy said, "Duck." Immediately afterwards the fine film of a waterfall covered her, shocked her out of the lethargy into which she had fallen.

They were stopping a great deal, and in each pause she vaguely saw Tracy's body bending forward in the saddle as if to penetrate the pall ahead. And each time they pressed on, his voice would run gently behind him. She knew he was reassuring her, buoying her up—the thoughtful act of a kindly man. Once, before she had known him, all his reported acts had made a different impression upon her. She had thought of him as wild and uncaring and a little ruthless. A supreme individualist, moved only by his own transient emotions. But it had been a false estimate. Beneath the hardness and the skepticism of Hugh Tracy was a fine gentility. It was an odd blending. In one day's time he could pound a man with his fists, intent on destruction; and in that same day he could speak to her as one who guarded something fragile. As brief as was her acquaintance with him, she had seen him act in the extremes of temper where the bottommost character of the man had stood naked; and so she thought she knew him as well as anybody ever would. The outward face of him was full of contradictions, cross-purposes, dark reflections; beneath lay an unerrant simplicity. It was her privilege to see this—not his. He never would know himself, for his type showed best in action and loved introspection not at all. One thing was as certain as the gleaming stars: he would never change, and the full-blooded energy in him would drive him relentlessly on to the end.

These thoughts rose in her slowly over the long interval, to provide a kind of anesthesia against the strain of the flight. Thrown back upon herself, she lost all sense of the passing hours, and thus at last woke with a start to find the forward motion stopped. Her pony stood jaded on the sightless trail; Tracy was gone. It was with some effort that she repressed the quick desire to call out and dispel the feeling of being utterly alone; yet she did, at last catching a sound of Tracy roving somewhere ahead. When he returned, it was to drift beside her, his shape quite blurred in the black.

"We camp here," he said.

Plainly there was a disappointment in his voice, and she fought back her weariness to answer him: "If you're worrying about me, don't. I can go on."

"Not now. We've traveled as far as we dare without sight of something. Follow me."

He went ahead slowly for perhaps a hundred yards and Lynn, close behind, felt some great shape envelop her. If anything, the density of the night increased. Tracy was down. His helping hand reached up to her and guided her to the uncertain ground. "Stay here," he murmured. He was away again, this time with the horses. Cold wind poured like water along some natural crevice to cut through the clothing; looking above, she saw a wider patch of sky, and from that judged they had reached a more open area. Tracy's murmured talk arrived ahead of him. He touched her and drew her with him. The bite of the wind suddenly ceased, and his words rang back with a hollow, dampered effect:

"Natural room in the side of the cliff. Duck your head, Lynn."

Her shoulder points scraped the jaws of a narrow aperture. Inside, she somehow felt that the ceiling of this vault swept away from her. Tracy led her on, placed her against a wall. "We can afford to have a little fire in here. I'll only be gone a moment."

But the moment stretched out dismally. The oddest of sounds filled this cavern, a subdued muttering and bubbling and groaning that appeared to rise from beneath her feet. Suppressing the instinctive fears such as every human feels in the presence of the unknown, Lynn put both hands against the wall and slowly swung her head from side to side. Then suddenly she got the meaning of that weird uneasiness and laughed silently at herself. It was nothing more than the wind currents playing across the mouth of the cavern and making a sort of vast musical jug out of it. Tracy tramped noisily along the corridor and entered the vault, dropping something on the floor.

"What I most dislike about passing up a few meals," said he, conversationally, "is the fact that you just miss that many times to enjoy one of the simple pleasures of a highly complicated life. I wouldn't swear to it, but I think we'll probably eat around tomorrow noon."

Matchlight burst the black, and a little raveling flame shot upward from an arranged pile of sage stems and pine branches. But the incipient fire immediately dropped to a sulky glow, finding no draught of air to fan it. Tracy tried again, grumbling to himself. Presently the pitch particles on the pine branches caught and sputtered, and the girl saw Tracy's face outlined in the thin blaze with a sort of saturnine thoughtfulness on it. Going over, she dropped to her knees and watched his fingers feeding in the more inflammable twigs.

"The Good Lord," went on Tracy, squinting at his chore, "provided a natural line rider's cabin here. But I doubt if there's anybody beside myself that knows of it. I ran into it one winter, badly needing some shelter."

"Won't the fire show, outside?"

"No. The passageway is crooked enough to block the light."

The blaze grew by fitful assaults on the wood. Tracy laid on half a dozen substantial broken jack-pine branches and went out again, presently returning with the saddles and saddle blankets. He laid both blankets neatly on the floor. "Your bed," said he. "And I'm sorry I forgot about the springs and mattress."

"One blanket for you," answered Lynn.

"I'll be outside, keeping an eye peeled," said Hugh after a studied silence.

Lynn rose suddenly and went around him. She took up one of the blankets, came back, and laid it on the floor, thus making two beds, one on either side of the fire. "Hugh," she said quietly, "you are not being as direct as I expect you to be. There's no need of a guard and you know it. The subterfuge isn't really necessary."

Hugh Tracy looked up to her. "There's only the fire between those two blankets, Lynn."

"Even that isn't necessary."

"I'm not so sure," muttered Tracy, staring into the heart of the flames. Oddly brusque, he went on. "It is better than midnight. And we'll have to be on our way by four o'clock. Better rest."

She sank down with a small amused sound of discomfort and

slowly pulled off her boots. "You'll sleep in here, Hugh, and I'll be the more comfortable for knowing it. Wouldn't it be silly of me to send you outside? I'm not an old maid."

Cross-legged by the heat, he rolled a cigarette and sorted out a glowing twig to light it. The girl struggled free from her coat, folded it for a pillow; she loosened the leg lacings of her riding breeches, pulled the blanket around her Indian fashion, and clasped her hands about her knees. Blood-red shadows danced shutter-like on the suggestion of walls to either side of them; yet seemingly they were in the core of a sphere that had no definite circumference. All that was tangible was the fire and these two people about it.

The girl watched Tracy's face, finding the rugged bronze of its surface overlaid by troubled imprints. Leaning forward, she spoke gently at him. "Never worry. What happens will happen. We have had the day together—and that is something, to me."

"Ahead of us," said Tracy reflectively, "is a bad piece. We've got within shouting distance of the desert. In the morning we'll have to cross—before clear daylight comes. It's only about a mile wide, and there's plenty of shelter on the farther edge. But we wasted a lot of time coming along the rough country, and it's likely Shadrow will have men posted out there now. That's why I didn't go on tonight. Couldn't afford to run into his crew on the trail."

"It's up to you. But will daylight be any better?"

"There's an old Apache trick of waiting till just before first light comes in the morning. Most Indians attacked at that hour, figuring the other side to be worn down to sleep. That's when we'll try. The TS crowd will be asleep—I hope."

"Otherwise we run and pray?"

"It's certain we'll run," drawled Hugh.

Silence came between them, and there was no sound save the wind plucking away at the mouth of the cavern and the slight hiss of the burning sticks. Tracy tossed his cigarette into the blaze, laid on the rest of the pine fragments. Light flashed against the gray surfaces of his eyes and turned all the squarish fighting features more indomitably stubborn. But the watching girl, etching all this picture of him into her memory, saw something she had not seen before—a hint of patience, a painstaking, hard-held patience created out of the unruly spirit that so habitually turned against this manner of mildness.

Tracy took to poking the ashes with a stem of sage. "Lynn, you have no relatives left, outside of Tade?"

"No."

"He has all your money?"

"Until I am twenty-three. Why?"

He shook his head, scowling at the flames. After a while the girl went on: "That's not your worry, Hugh. It is mine. I am perfectly capable of making my own way in the world. Who do you suppose ran my father's hotel and his business affairs? He didn't. He spent the days dreaming. I have worked hard. I can again. Now quit thinking of it."

A little show of amusement appeared on his face. "Tade's got no kin except you. Ever stop to think, Lynn, that unless he wills it formally otherwise, you're the inheritor of that ranch?"

"What an encouraging thought!" said the girl. "Have you a pencil and such a thing as a paper?"

He produced the pencil readily, but searched himself at length for the paper, finally producing a rectangular slip which he passed over with an accompanying explanation. "Long time ago I took that blank check and started for Antelope to buy some cows, which was to be the beginning of my own ranchin' ventures. I never reached Antelope. They nailed me with a .30-.30 from the rim, and Bill Vivian found me six hours later, same as dead. That was the shot which set off all this. And the check's still blank. Always will be now."

She made a few stray lines on the clear side and suddenly gave over the attempt. Unconsciously she put these things beside her blanket instead of giving them back to him. "Good-night, Hugh."

For the first time this last hour, he allowed himself a full and free glance at her. The ash hair lay loosely beautiful on her head, and she sat with her small, definite shoulders a little forward while the firelight brought out the robust, alluring symmetry of her throat and breast. The languor of physical weariness softened her face. Heavy-lidded, her eyes met his squarely with the oddest of lights in them, enigmatic and warm; and her lips were drawn half apart, smiling.

"Good-night," said Tracy.

Suddenly she held out her hand and he took it, gripped it and leaned forward, seeing the pulse in the hollow of her throat beat more swiftly.

"Lynn——" he muttered, and bore down on himself with all the iron pressure of his will. "I warned you," he said, roughly.

Her hand remained still; all her body was quiet.

"There's something in your mind," said Tracy and waited for an answer, black head bent toward her, doggedly trying to read what was in her face. Yet what he found was elusive, smilingly

113

hidden. And finally he drew back his hand. Her own dropped to the blanket. She said, gravely:

"I was wondering if I could believe you when you said that you took nothing by force—that nothing gained by force was permanent. Well, Hugh, I do believe you—now." Lying back, she pulled the folded coat under her head, wrapped the blanket around her. Hugh leaned forward to fold it across her feet. The gray-blue regard reached up to him slantwise, almost closed out by her heavy lids.

"Lynn," he muttered, "never do that again. It might have turned out another way."

"So? Yet it didn't, Hugh, and this is the happy end of an unhappy day. You've a right to spank me. But I'll sleep soundly, knowing you're here. Wake me when you want."

She was asleep as soon as the words were spoken, half curled in the blanket and one hand stretched toward him. Over the dying fire, Tracy watched the faintly smiling face until the light grew dim. Afterwards he reached for his own blanket and put it over her. Bolt upright, he waited out the laggard day.

CHAPTER 12

···•——◆——•···

THE FILLED CHECK

THAT last hour before dawn, when the courage and vitality of man ebb furthest out and the banked fires of life sink lowest, was perhaps the most miserable experience Hugh Tracy ever had endured. It was his third night of sleeplessness, save for an intermittent catnap or so; it was the fifth since he had set himself against the outgoing tide of fortune. Like most riding men, he had little surplus tissue to use. Strong as he was, the intense activity of his body immediately broke up the energy supplied it by food; and without food the physical engines swiftly fell to idling speed. So now he suffered the inevitable consequences of his fasting. Worn ragged, along with his responsibilities, he was bitterly assailed by the hosts of defeat and futility; and in this hour they were hard to shake off. All he could do was bite his teeth together and wait, summon up that patience of which he possessed so little and stare into blackness like some East Indian fanatic undergoing scarification of the flesh. Nor was anything in all his career as enormously relieving as the sight of the first faint light breaking through the vault's aperture.

Instantly he rose, stiff and sore from his cold vigil, and went out. Actually there was no daylight yet but only a graying of the densely packed shadows. Great clouds of mist rolled sluggishly through the canyon, faintly to be seen, striking him with a perceptible impact and leaving a film of dampness on his face. Rolling a cigarette, he tried three matches before one would stay lighted in the emulsified rain. Gradually, very gradually at first, the rims of the canyon began to shape up, rather low and comparatively far apart. Above the mists was an expanding brightness.

This last fact warned him to be on the move. Once the morning started to break, it would come with a rush, summer's full rose dawn pouring out of the east. Turning down to another part of the canyon, he got his tethered ponies—blanketed with dew—and brought them back; and going into the vault, he woke the girl.

"Another day, Lynn. Starlight's soon gone."

It mildly astonished him to see how swiftly she woke, and how alertly. Those brief hours of repose seemed enough to fill that slim, splendid body with force again. She came upright in the blankets, face a luminous and blurred oval before him, and her talk broke along the dismal cavern with a brisk gayety. "Hugh," she said, "did you ever give our poor cave ancestors a thought? No wonder the men went out and slew the saber-tooth with clubs and stones. After this sort of a bed, I feel half a savage myself."

"Bad night?"

"No. Wonderful night. I went down and down and down to the bottom of creation and never stirred. Even dreamed of wonderful things."

"As how?"

"That all was to be well. There was an ending, a fine ending. I was standing in a peach orchard, eating like a pig. I guess that's why it seemed such a good dream. I never did, in all my life, have enough peaches to eat."

"I can appreciate the fruit," he drawled, "but a black pot full of coffee would hit me better."

"What do you expect of a dream?" asked Lynn, rising. "You want these blankets, don't you?"

He took them, caught up the gear, and went out to saddle the horses. In that short space of time the curling mists were beginning to show cotton edges and had perceptibly thinned. Long as he had been in the country, he never ceased to be surprised at the sudden march of day; and now he realized that it would be a toss-up whether or not he reached the desert strip while the dusk remained. When the girl came out, he said as much. "We'll just make it—barely make it."

Mounted, she bent forward to see him more clearly. "You didn't sleep, Hugh."

"Afraid to. Ordinarily I can set my mind at any hour and wake within ten minutes of the time. But not unless I've had the normal amount of sleep under my belt. In that respect I'm a little short-weighted to date. Here we go."

He struck southward again. There was the beginning of a long grade, and to left and right the canyon walls ran increasingly lower. Water boiled out of a rock spring; a four-foot rattler lay full length on the trail, touching off the ponies.

"An omen, if you're looking for one," murmured Hugh. They came to the top of the grade, out of the long canyon at last. A belt of timber was to the fore, and the trail struck directly into it. Beyond the tree tops was the promise of a sweeping open. But to the west the trees ran up another small butte, a vantage point of some consequence. Hugh led that way, finding the ground clear enough to advance on the trot until the incline grew sharply severe. Within a hundred yards they were above the fog wreaths. The girl, looking eastward through a break in the pines, spoke quietly: "Another clear, hot day coming, Hugh, there's always a promise in the morning."

Tracy looked around, smiling slightly, and then drove ahead, up the last fold of the butte. They made slow time through a dense growth of brush and were wet to the skin when they finally halted on the butte's bald top. Anyway but westward they had a clear view of the world; and here for the first time Lynn saw the southern desert strip which began at the very foot of the butte. Perhaps a mile beyond that flat surface the looming sides of another hill series stood half concealed in the shadows. To the east—all along the rim of the far-flung Powder—was a widening crack of clear violet light.

Tracy had crossed the open and now stood facing the northern sweep of timber—that area out of which they had come. "Lynn," he called.

The girl swung about and cantered to where he was. He lifted a pointing arm, and she saw without further explanation what he meant. Over there in a clearing the crimson wedge of a morning fire split the twilight.

"It's Shadrow—twenty minutes behind us and in no hurry."

"Well?"

"I said he was in no hurry. If he was he'd be on the rustle by now. But he's made a point of lighting that fire for us to see. We won't go that way, will we? We'll head for the desert. He knows that. He's all ready for it."

"You really believe he has men out in the desert?"

"Certain of it. Either on this edge in the trees, or else on the far edge."

"No other way we can go?"

"Not now," said Hugh.

The girl looked at him a long while, a certain quiet concentration in her eyes. "It is you they'll shoot at, Hugh. Not me."

"The last run," he reflected, "is out there. Not so much of a run and soon over. Beyond, we're safe. Shadrow can't drag his men any farther from TS without leaving his headquarters unguarded. It's a guessing game, and our guess is as good as his. He can't tell at just what point we leave this line of timber. So if he's posted some of the crew it's more likely they'll be on the opposite side, watching us come. I'm going to walk down the slope and have a look before we start."

The girl nodded, clouded thoughtfulness across her brow. Tracy looked up at her quickly. "Afraid of it, Lynn?"

"For you."

"That's out. They've tried for me too many times. Their luck's gone. Wait right here."

He walked away in long strides and soon fell down the slope, losing sight of her as the trees took him. The trail dropped sharply, dipped into a ravine and out again. Four hundred yards brought him to the sandy margin of the desert floor; and, paused there beside a tree trunk, he made his survey of the roundabout area. It was, he realized, not much of a reconnaissance and reassured him only to the extent of the immediate vicinity. Backed up by his hunch in the matter, he decided that Shadrow had not placed any of the hands at this initial point of departure. Out on the desert he could find nothing suggestive. "No," he mused, "it's the way I figured. He'll have his dogs crawlin' yonder at the foot of that ridge—watching me come." There was nothing to be done about it, and no more calculation could help; so thinking, he turned back at the half-run.

He had wasted a good quarter-hour, and the pale eastern glow was gradually coming upon the land. On the edge of the butte's bald space he halted dead.

Only his horse stood there. The girl and her horse had gone.

"Lynn."

The echo beat back from the glistening green margin of the timber of the clearing and warned him to be still. Waiting a moment—a quick alarm spreading through him—he listened into that deep silence for some other rumor of sound, some disturbance of brush. Yet the moments fled and nothing materialized. Then his turning glance reached as far as the pony to discover Lynn's felt hat hanging on the saddle horn. That put him to instant motion. Rushing forward, he seized the hat; as he did so a dislodged slip of paper eddied gently to the earth.

He knew then what had happened. Even as he reached down he understood that this act of the girl's had been thought over last night in the vault, thought over and prepared for. That slip was the blank check he had given her; on the reverse side of it this was written:

MY DEAR:

"You should have seen this last night. It was what I was trying to tell you. All of my love and all of me—as long as you ever shall want me. No matter what happens,

118

*you have a right to know that. But there is no other
way—and this seems the only decent thing for me to do.
Should anything happen to you I could never, never
smile again.*

"Lynn."

He was instantly in the saddle, racing for the northern edge of
the butte. But on the point of dipping down its far slope, he
reined in. From this eminence he could see three or four trails
winding through the trees, and on none of them did Lynn appear.
She had gone on, into the deeper timber; and by now must be
halfway to Shadrow's campfire. "Lord love her," he muttered,
" she has done the wrong thing, trying to help me."

For it was all very clear to him. She would go to Shadrow to
check the pursuit, to argue with her uncle, to take away at least
half of the man's reason for being on the trail. These were her
aims—and she would fail in them. Inevitably she would fail, not
knowing Shadrow's basic character. The TS owner would never
stop, once having come this near to success. Moreover, Lynn's
appearance would be a sure sign of how near at hand the game
was. It would not stop Shadrow. It would put him in motion so
much the sooner.

"And she was thinking I could ride away, to come and fight
another day," said Tracy, staring up to the brightening sky.
"No. There is no new deal. Can't be and won't be. He's got her
again, for whatever he pleases to do. Now I've got to hit
back—quick."

Across the still air rolled a report that went flattening away
along the corridors of this rough land; and as if it were a signal
for him instead of for others—which he knew it to be—he swung
across the butte's top and quartered down in the direction of that
canyon out of which he had earlier brought Lynn. "Tade," he
muttered, "is notifying the surrounding scouts to be up and
hunting." Then, twenty feet forward on his course, he sharply
checked, once more arrested by the long reach of two rifle
echoes. One seemed to rise out of the canyon below; the other
came from the opposite side of the butte, more remotely placed.
Whatever his improvised plan, he discarded it now; no clearer
signal could have told him that he was boxed in on at least three
sides of the butte. His original thinking had been right—there
was but one way out, and that ahead, across the desert. Wheeling,
he descended to the very margin of the desert. All the overlying
shadows were breaking, and the farther hills were suddenly and
blackly definite against the horizon. Glancing to left and to right,

119

Hugh rode from the protecting trees and aimed for a fissure in those hills a mile away.

Even as he left shelter behind he understood clearly what was to come about. This was sound sagebrush hunting. Having driven him from cover, which was the culmination of their long campaign, they could now crack down. But for the moment, this general conviction was split into sections of worry; and his strongest worry was for his exposed rear. Along the near edge of timber just left behind, an ambushed gun might well enough reach him. Crouched in the saddle, he played the horse for all that it would give, instantly feeling that the beast was beaten before it started. being a TS animal—the one he had taken from the ranch porch—it sufffered the usual Shadrow practice of underfeeding and had further been punished by the last thirty hours of hard usage. There was no freshness in the pony, its stride was ragged, and already it began to draw deeply for wind. Meanwhile, Tracy's screwed-up attention failed to catch the half-expected detonation out of the rear. Looking about, he saw only the unbroken fringes of the trees, some three or four hundred yards away by now; and a little reassured, he pulled up to a canter, nursing what little reserve there was in his mount for a contingency he expected to develop before much more time elapsed. At this pace, he gained the long furrow of a small arroyo, dipped into it, and rose out again.

Beyond it, halfway over the flat, he saw them coming at him.

It was exactly as he believed and feared. Considerably to the rightward of that fissure toward which he bent his flight, and perhaps a thousand yards distant, six riders spilled from shelter and drove diagonally across the desert for him. Directly across his path rose a sudden-ripped jet of dust and afterwards a rifle's laggard report reached out. That was long-distance shooting—and from behind. Twisting, he discovered a pair of horsemen following from the canyon country at a dead tilt. Thus his position was, bracketed and unsheltered, cut off from protection either way. It was, he thought again with the old heedless anger drumming up in him, exactly as he had believed and feared. The men of Powder, versed in all the shrewd tricks of warfare, had performed the logical surround of quarry.

A second puff of dust streaked the desert, more off-target than the first had been, and again the echo came from behind. Those following two were trying for the odd chance of a hit at a moving bull's-eye better than nine hundred yards distant. But these men he ruled out of his mind immediately. Reaching forward to the saddle boot, he drew up his rifle. At the same time he rowled the pony to a full run, shifting to a more easterly course. The oncoming six saw the maneuver and adjusted themselves accordingly; and for a space of time it became a parallel running fight that forced him deeper and deeper into the desert's open strip and put those hills he was trying to reach the farther away. Compactly stated, they had him entirely in their hands. Meanwhile he detected a slight inward shift on their part, and this he could not match without being thrown back on the rear two who potted away regardless of luck. He thought once of facing about and charging that pair, taking his chances on getting back to the canyon country again. But it was only a brief thought and soon discarded. Behind the pair, he realized, all of Shadrow's group somewhere advanced.

"I'll follow my nose," he muttered and hooked the reins about the saddle horn. Lifting his rifle, he began a raking attack on the outstretched party of six. His first shot fell useless and unseen in the distance. The second appeared to land directly beneath a horse, for the animal pitched high and bucked crazily, jamming up the following riders. Tracy pumped a third shell into the chamber and held his fire, at once realizing he played the part of a sucker. That group closed on him yard by yard, his own horse was beginning to tremble with exhaustion, and the bullets smacked out of the rear with a closer effect. They were fooling with him, and all he actually did now was spar against the sure finish. The thought went through him like fire, and his swelling temper exploded. "By God," he swore, "I never win playin' patient! Now we'll see who caves in first!" He brought the pony sharply out of its paralleling course and aimed straight for the bunch.

At the most it was a narrow six hundred yards, and they hadn't yet gone for their rifles. Wondering about that, he opened up, savagely trying for the hit. His last bullet found one. A horse buckled at the knees and went plunging down, throwing its rider in a high and whirling arc through the air. It checked the others. The whole line whipped around, swept back to the fallen man and screened him for a passing moment. Thumbing fresh cartridges into the gun, he saw them bunch up. A yelling talk crossed the prairie and a quick-flung curse came after. Two men spurred up to the prone figure and dismounted, dropping flat to the earth. The other three wheeled and charged. Gone stone-cold, nothing left in his mind but the overmastering desire to destroy, Hugh dragged his pony back on its haunches and jumped down. Prone, he leveled the sights full on the most advanced of those three and held the aim a long second. The two who had dug in by the fallen man were opening up a steady fire. Dust banners made a powdered fog beside him; his horse grunted, struggled away, and fell. And his squeezing finger drove a bullet into the yonder rider. That rider pitched out of the saddle without a sound. The others bent low and curved to get around Tracy, who tried again, missed his mark, and then aimed for a horse. It was a good shot. The horse fell; the unsaddled hand lay as if stunned.

It left the remaining rider alone against the skyline, and that fact appeared to dishearten him. His reaction was to wheel away, throw himself Indian fashion far over to one side of the mount, and race back. Meanwhile the dumped fellow lay flattened and took up the argument with his revolver futilely. Tracy, thinking of the two hands who followed him out of the canyon country, turned to see where they were, and caught only the tops of their ponies showing above the small arroyo some distance behind.

Steadying himself to the frontal attack again, he was astonished by a series of spanging echoes crossing the flat from the southern hills—from the shelter he was striving to reach. It was a heavy and increasing fire, and he saw its effect instantly, the dropping lead beating up dust whorls about the riflemen who had elected to fortify themselves by the one who had first been pitched from his saddle. At that, the lone fellow left mounted made a complete circle as if essaying to catch the direction of this new attack. He cried out something to the others and then fled—cutting a detour around Tracy and striking out for the canyon country behind. Tracy hugged his gun butt and riveted his attention on the TS riflemen, whose attack abruptly fell off. He saw them crouched half on their knees.

"Running," he muttered. "All right, that's fair." He held his bullet, giving them the chance. Both sprang up at the same time and raced for the waiting ponies. They were asaddle the next moment, following the lead of the first retreating hand. Those far guns in the hills bore down with a malicious purpose, all the dust whorls jetting up short of the fugitives.

Out of this furious mêlée had come a break of luck. The horse of that rider he had fairly hit stood now directly to the fore, reins down. Casting up his accounts rapidly, Tracy decided to run for the animal. Beforehand, however, he looked behind again and saw that those two in the arroyo were swiftly departing from it, bound back to the canyon country. So, save for the unhorsed fellow now banging away with the revolver, he was in the clear. Tracy bellowed out: "You'll never reach me with that! Go on—leg it! I'll hold my fire!'' But the man's hat made a stubborn wagging from side to side. He refused to move.

"He's thinking," reflected Tracy, "that I'll do a Spanish on him. That's what he'd do, in my shoes. Well——" He bit off the remark and cursed at himself. "No. He's figuring Shadrow's bunch will be here in a minute."

He looked around once more and discovered the guess was right. Over beneath the outline of the same butte from which he had earlier departed, a long line of riders broke into the clear and came dusting on. Tracy lifted himself to his feet and made a rush for the idle pony.

The lone TS hand turned on the earth and aimed at the horse with his revolver, clearly meaning to kill it. Tracy yelled violently at him: "Stop that, you fool!" and came to a stand, whipping up the rifle. The man saw that gesture from the corner of his eyes and abruptly switched his aim again, trying for Tracy. It was two hundred yards and no distance for a short piece; yet he tried. Deliberately aiming, he took up the trigger slack. But he never let the bullet go. The man suddenly put both elbows on the sand, throwing his gun away. At that, Tracy wheeled and renewed his rush for the horse. One rear glance found Shadrow's party half across the desert.

The firing from the hills had stopped, leaving a strange silence after all the rolling echoes had played through the brightening morning. Running to within fifty feet of the riderless pony, Tracy dropped to a walk and went on with a murmured reassurance. He expected a bolt, but the pony, trained to stand on dropped reins, only fiddled about those two hanging bits of leather. Tracy strode on, seized them. He was in the leather and away. Suddenly a long firing beat out of the hills again. Behind was a ragged shouting and a fusillade from Shadrow's crew. Tracy bent down and aimed the pony's ears for that fissure he had been so stubbornly trying to reach. Flanking a pile of rock rubble, he struck up a short incline. Jack pines flashed by, and then the green tall timber of the ridge came down to meet him. There was a clear trail leading on to the heights. In that trail stood Bill Vivian. Tracy pulled up.

"Well," said Vivian with a deceptive, conversational calm, "it's me that always pulls you out of a jackpot. Don't you never learn, Mister Tracy?"

"So you're here?" grunted Hugh.

"Who in thunder did you expect?" retorted Vivian. "Where else ought I be?"

Tracy scowled at the little man out of his heavy, red-rimmed

123

eyes. "Off pickin' daisies, you mug. That's where I usually find you."

Bill Vivian gave voice to a short and disparaging phrase and looked across the desert. "If that bunch means to come this way, we've got to get on the boat. Follow me, Hugh. The boys are up in the brush."

"Hold on," said Tracy, watching the yonder space closely. Shadrow's crew spread into the shallow arroyo which marked the middle of the desert strip and halted there. The unhorsed rider went running back, waving his arms. Eastward, a long flare of sunlight burst over the rim, and the world began to assume a still and harsh and burning aspect. Shadow and brightness alternately cut the distant rugged country into jagged sections; all the desert turned to a white glare. The unhorsed rider reached Shadrow's main party, stood beside a mounted figure, and talked with a continued gesturing. Then the mounted figure spurred forward, alone. Presently he halted and turned back. One fist shook skyward.

"Something," mused Vivian, "seems to be wrong with his army."

A long pause followed, after which the whole line of hands came out of the arroyo and cantered ahead. Then, from the timbered section directly above Tracy, a blast of concerted firing rushed out and shattered the pervading stillness. Attention still pinned to Shadrow's party, Hugh saw the sudden dust whorls dappling the desert around that deploying line. The effect of the firing was instant. The foremost man wheeled and threw his arm overhead, at which the whole line reversed itself and surged back for the canyon country. Nobody paid any attention to the TS fellow afoot. All the riders swept by him and he followed on the trot.

"The rewards of faithfulness," muttered Tracy, watching the man stumble through the shot-sprayed dust.

Bill Vivian struck out a disappointed oath. "There goes the chance I figured was ours. Hell's pit!"

"Now just how was it you knew I might be this far south?" demanded Hugh.

"We was on the high point by Dead Axle grade and we saw a fire burnin' over by the butte early this morning. So, havin' picked up part of Shadrow's trail yesterday—we been scoutin' steady since you left TS on the run—we made the good guess you was bein' chased over here. Well, we made it down from Dead Axle in forty minutes and got here in time to see you come into the flat. You sure tipped our hand. We figured you'd make it here with the hounds on your heels. That would've been fine. We could of pinched them in on the trail here. But it was sure news to us that some more TS hogheads were hidin' on this side. When they came out to cramp you down we had to take steps."

"How did you know Shadrow was on my heels or that I'd left TS on the run?"

"One of Tade's men deserted him yesterday and rode to Antelope to spread the news. We had a fellow in Antelope listenin' for dope. He came right on and told us."

Hugh grumbled. "Who in thunder is 'we'?"

"Follow me," grinned Bill Vivian, and scrambled up the stiff side of the trail. Hugh followed slowly, leading his horse. Through a fringe of pines, he came upon a semi-circular clearing that faced the desert. And on the edges of the clearing, flattened on the dirt and faced out in the direction of the now disappearing Shadrow bunch, lay ten dusty figures.

"Here's the pilgrim," said Vivian laconically.

They turned then and Hugh, looking along that row of slim and reckless cheeks, felt a deep stirring of emotion, a quick lightness of heart. These were men he knew. They were his friends, his riding partners of old. They were his kind. He cleared his throat and looked away from them.

"You're a tough-looking set of sand fleas," he muttered. "Where've you been for three months?"

"Gaze upon 'em," gloated Bill. "When I left you on the spur the other night I proceeded to all the hide-outs in this country. I got 'em. You bet I got 'em. Morally, they ain't worth a damn. A more sinful collection of monkeys you never laid eyes on. But here they are, Hugh—the best of a bad lot. Sabe Venner's lost flesh since you seen him last."

One slender giant rose up with a broad grin. "What big teeth you got, Grammaw. Hugh, Lord bless your homely self. Welcome—and now that we're duly assembled and constituted, what's next in this giddy whirl?"

Bill Vivian made a vulger sound with his lips. "It's always like this, dammit. I ain't general no more when Hugh comes around."

"Shadrow," said Hugh, watching the far hills, "is going home. That's certain. He's finished with this chase. He'll be back at TS by noon, cooking up another mess of hell."

"Say," put in Bill Vivian, "where's the girl you was supposed to've kidnapped?"

"How did you know that?"

"It's all over the Powder."

"She went back to Shadrow," said Tracy slowly. "To help me."

"Trust a woman to gum up the works."

Tracy, weary and irritable, said gruffly: "Shut up, Bill. Your knowledge of human nature is only exceeded by your Christian benevolence. But does Powder know anything about Bat Testervis being in that kidnapping?"

"Why, no," answered Bill, full of interest. "Was he?"

"That's odd," murmured Hugh. "Is there anything to eat in this outfit?"

Sabe Venner moved forward. "Eatin' breakfast is next up. Somebody start a fire while I hack off the bacon."

"By God," grunted Hugh, slowly settling full length on the ground, "I'm tired. Have to get an hour's sleep. Punch me when that bacon's ready."

"This will interest you," said Bill Vivian. "We've found out that things ain't going so well on TS. This man that left 'em went on to say that there wasn't no more than forty hands——"

Sabe Venner bent over Hugh and looked curiously into the latter's face. "He's asleep, Bill. Dead as a doorknob."

All those grave-eyed hands walked up and stared at the prostrate Hugh. "I've seen him plenty," reflected Sabe, "but, by Jodey, I never seen him like that. Never thought he had a limit."

Bill Vivian unsaddled a horse swiftly and got the blanket. He laid it over Hugh and looked around him with a slant-eyed severity. "You lousebound eggs, be quiet. We stick here till noon, see? He sleeps till noon."

"Well," Sabe Venner wanted to know, "what'll we do then?"

"He'll have a damned good idea when he wakes up," prophesied Bill. "He always does. Meanwhile I guess I'm still general. There's got to be a scout put out on top of Dead Axel grade. And somebody's got to slide over Mogul and look down into Antelope. You, Sabe. And Willy Bones. Willy for the Antelope business. He knows Shadrow soil best."

CHAPTER 13

FIRE BURNS FROM THE CENTER

AT NOONING Shadrow returned to TS with his crew and Lynn Isherwood. The girl immediately dismounted and disappeared inside the house; as for the men, they halted there in the sultry baking heat of that ugly plaza and waited Shadrow's word. Hungry, caked with trail dust, they stared at the owner sullenly. The cook of the outfit came from the kitchen, saw the arrivals, and returned to his pots, muttering. A hand—one of the guards left to protect the quarters—walked slowly from the bunkhouse.

Shadrow's face was the color of clay and putty. Deep lines slashed his slack skin, his lip corners curved cruelly downward, and when he stepped to the ground it was with an air of physical infirmity quite noticeable to the group. But presently he drew up his rickety shoulders and pushed his odd head forward to return the massed inspection. A blaze of insolent temper poured out of the red-flecked eyes; and suddenly the heat of that wrath hit them. "You're a sick-lookin' bunch of whelps! Don't stand there and gawk! Get the hell out of my sight! Leave your horses saddled!"

The members of the crew shifted toward the racks, dismounted, and ambled off to the bunkhouses. Tolbert and Maunders remained with the old man, who threw his gaunt glare at them. "A miserable, yellow pack of hounds! Not worth the powder to blow 'em to hell! I'd give half my fortune to be thirty years younger. By God, I'd take Hugh Tracy's trail alone—and I'd knock him down!"

"You been pushin' the boys pretty hard, with blamed little consideration," observed Maunders.

"Bah," snorted Shadrow. "They're sick sheep!"

"Sure. You'd like to have us walk right into Tracy and get the lead," grumbled Maunders. "Well, some of the lads did exactly that. And they'll ride no more. When a man's workin' for thirty dollars a month, it don't seem so swell to butt into a gun."

Shadrow lashed out at him: "Shut up! You're the worst bungler in the lot! I ain't got a man I can put trust in! Ain't a one of them with his heart in my affairs! It's a hell of a situation to consider every blasted one of you'd cut my throat!" Wheeling, he stamped into the office. Maunders looked slyly at Tolbert; and together they slowly followed through the doorway. Shadrow was in the act of pouring himself a drink. "It ain't natural, it ain't reasonable," he burst out. "I'm the strongest man in this country. I can whip any other outfit. I can do exactly as I damned well please. I've got the biggest crew and the most money. And still, by thunder, I can't nail Hugh Tracy in his tracks! What's the matter with us?"

Maunders took up a slow pacing of the room, his dull blackened face stolidly set. The slate eyes flashed over to Shadrow, who downed his drink and looked ominously at his lieutenants. "I can give you two pretty good reasons," muttered Maunders.

"Can, hey?" snapped Shadrow, heavy with sarcasm. "Well, let's have the due fruit of your massive intellect. Go on, tell me."

"For one thing," said Maunders stubbornly, "Tracy's got your ticket."

"What in the name of creation does that mean?" yelled Shadrow. Outraged beyond measure, he swept all the accumulated papers off his desk with one hand.

"It's a book," insisted Maunders. "He's got your ticket. You never will get him because you wasn't borned to get him. That's what I mean. The deck don't cut that way. The bullet ain't in your gun that's goin' to hit him. Maybe you think you're the biggest bull buffalo on the prairie. You ain't. Tracy is."

"Go on," said Shadrow, with the same taunting, malign temper. "What else?"

Maunders's own throttled anger began to rise into his talk. "Confound you, Shadrow. You talk of the crew bein' yellow and of wantin' to cut your throat! Well, half of that's true enough. You've got no loyalty comin' to you anyhow. Why should you have? You treat all of us like dung under your feet. You suppose a man is going to take a bust in the nose from you and then go out and lay himself open to a killin' because you want him to? Sure, you got money. What of it? There ain't a ranch in the West that feeds as lousy, drives as hard, pays as little, or is as downright gloomy to work for as this one."

"You lost your nerve a week ago," gibed Shadrow. "You're through."

"Don't tell me when I'm through!" shouted Maunders. "You better sing humble! You've lost a lot of men at Tracy's hands, and you'll lose more. Don't make any mistake about that. There ain't so many of us standin' between Tracy and you. I'm one of the few—and you've got little license to tell me where I head in!''

"We run him out of the country," growled Shadrow, filling up his glass again. "He'll never dare to show around Powder again."

Lake Tolbert stood, as always, in a corner, lank frame slouched against the wall. He broke his inscrutable silence for the first time:

"You're wrong, Tade. He'll be back."

Shadrow jerked his head about as if stung. "Another county heard from! You're supposed to be the best tracker in the state. Well, I'll say you're overrated. You lost Tracy's trail half a dozen times." Bending forward, the slack and caviling face fixed on the foreman, he said slowly: "What's the matter, Lake? You losin' your nerve too?"

"What would you think?" droned Tolbert.

The air of the room was packed with hostility, the threat of eruption. Maunders backed away and glanced over at Tolbert with a concentrating interest. Ready enough to talk, he held his tongue now. This was something new—this recrimination and accusation and bickering between the owner and the foreman. Shadrow's lewdly evil eyes sharpened—dangerous sign—and his lips turned bloodlessly thin. Tolbert's returning stare was fixed in an unchanged, unmoved blankness. All this held on for a matter of moments, and was broken by Shadrow, who reached down to his filled glass and drank the liquor at a gulp.

"He never will dare to put his foot inside of Powder again," repeated Shadrow.

"He'll be knocking at your door soon enough," replied Tolbert.

"My sentiments exactly," added Maunders.

"Why?" cried the badgered Shadrow. "How can he? What with? How? Answer me that!"

Maunders almost smiled. With an evident sarcasm he prompted Tolbert: "You tell him, Lake."

"Because he's a fighter," said Tolbert slowly. "Because, when he gets his mind made up, he's like a bull on the charge. Never considerin' whether he'll stand or fall." And after a moment's thought he added: "Pretty hard to stop a man that won't be stopped."

"He'll never get far," said Shadrow. "He's alone."

"He'll have help," said Tolbert with the same calm.

Shadrow's aggravation increased; he cursed passionately. "Not enough help to amount to a tinker's dam! Look here, Lake, I've

129

got this country under my little finger. Nobody dares to buck me."

But Tolbert shook his head slowly. "And that's why he'll have help. You've run your power high, wide, and handsome and never given anybody a break. A lot of people hate you, Tade. All that keeps 'em from workin' on you is fear. When they see a man like Tracy come fighting back, they'll join him. And he'll be knocking at your door. Make up your mind to it."

"A fight, uh?" growled Shadrow. "All right. I'll see Mister Tracy accommodated. I'll lick him so bad and I'll lick this country so bad no man will ever dare look me in the face again. Fine! It's what I want!"

The other two said nothing. Shadrow sat down, eyes like rubies against the sagging, dead-colored skin. Suddenly he raised his voice: "Lynn!" And after a moment he shouted her name again: "Lynn—come in here!"

"And that's another reason Hugh Tracy will be back," said Tolbert, the words tightening curiously.

"How's that?" asked Shadrow.

"You fool," said Tolbert, almost roughly, "those two people——"

"Oh," said Shadrow and fell silent, devouring the new thought. "So that's it? That's why she came back and made such a play to have me draw off. I didn't quite see it then. Fond of him, uh?" Slowly the cast of the man's face changed to a sly and malicious humor. A chuckle spilled out of his spindling chest; the lips pursed themselves on a grim, smirking smile. "Well, I know the answer to that."

The door opened from the living room, and Lynn Isherwood came reluctantly in. Shadrow said: "Get out of here, boys. I'm talkin' to this fine lady that eats TS chuck and still tries to do it hurt. Go on—get out of here!"

Maunders went out with a rolling swagger of his burly shoulders; but Tolbert clung to his place, more and more reserved of expression, until Shadrow's brittle words bit him again: 'What's the matter, Lake? Understand American, don't you?"

At that Tolbert crossed the place quite slowly and went through the door. Just beyond, he turned to look at the girl standing straight and calm in her place. Maunders grumbled, "Come on, Lake." Over by the bunkhouse all the crew stood in a thick circle. Talk rose in heated gusts; the two men walked that way, both preoccupied.

Shadrow sat hunched over his desk, heavy satisfaction still playing over the thin countenance; he stared at Lynn a long moment, one hand tapping restlessly on the desk top. When he finally broke the silence, it was with a snapping abruptness: "What made you break away from Tracy and come back to me?"

"Never mind," said the girl. "It didn't help me to come back."

"You bet it didn't. I was wonderin' if Tracy sent you back to ease the blow."

"You know better."

"So you wanted to help him pretty bad? Fond of the man, hey? Lost your fool head on him."

"Yes," said Lynn. "Yes."

"It will do no good," said Shadrow. "He's gone from here, and he won't be comin' back."

She made no answer to that. Prying at her face with his jealous, brilliant eyes, Shadrow beat another question against her: "Was that getaway arranged between you two beforehand? You planned to skip this ranch with him deliberate?"

Lynn's attention seemed to sharpen on the man. A knitted frown appeared above her eyes. "Whatever way it happened—it makes no difference to you."

"Look here, girl, there's something damned funny about it all," scolded Shadrow. "I never knew you was acquainted with Tracy. Was you?"

"Yes."

"Then," cried Shadrow, "you been stealin' off to his place unbeknowst to me! That's where you been ridin' lately, hey?"

"Yes."

"Nice—very nice!" muttered Shadrow, and the everchanging expression revealed something that turned Lynn's face to sudden scarlet.

"You," she said rapidly, "are rotten all the way through. I've seen a lot of scoundrels in my life, Tade, but none as mean, as contemptible as you."

"I see what I see," answered Shadrow, sardonically amused. "You're a woman and no different from any other woman. Nor you ain't the first girl that's thrown herself at Tracy. But it will do you no good. He ain't comin' back."

"I wouldn't be too sure of that," retorted Lynn.

The man bent forward, fully alert again. "What makes *you* so sure about it?"

"I know Hugh."

"Do, hey? Well, if he comes he'll get knocked over or taken.

I'm seeing to that. If he's taken he'll get life for murder or kidnappin'.''

"You couldn't make the charges stick!" flamed the girl.

'This is my country, you little fool," Shadrow answered contemptuously. "Antelope is my town. It is my court, my sheriff, my judge and my jury."

Lynn turned silent. Shadrow moved restlessly around in his chair, squinting upward at her with the same sly, worldly wisdom. "Still something funny about this. You made a powerful lot of noise getting out of here with Tracy the other night. You screamed. What for?"

The girl's air of puzzlement came back to her. She drew a breath, started to speak, and checked the impulse. Then, again changing her mind, she said: "Didn't you know? Bat Testervis was hiding out there beyond the yard. Hugh and I didn't know it. Bat caught me and got away. Hugh didn't catch up till the next morning."

Shadrow's eyes narrowed. "Then what happened?"

"Hugh fought him and drove him away."

"Early yesterday morning?"

"Yes."

"And there was a shot?"

"No," said the girl.

Shadrow fell to drumming the desk with his fingers, scowling. "Where?"

"By the cabin—just beyond the tall peak."

"Still funny," grunted Shadrow. "There was a shot somewhere around that country about then. Well"—and he squared himself toward her—"it makes no difference. You might as well put Tracy out of your head. He's through with the Powder whether he knows it or not. Now you listen to me. You've ate my bread and turned around to bite me. If you was a man I'd hide you proper. I would. But you're a woman—not to be trusted farther'n my little finger reaches. Never was a woman you could trust. I've had 'em trick me before."

"I don't wonder," said Lynn.

"How's that?" challenged Shadrow.

"Trickery brings trickery. It's all you know. You haven't got a friend in this world."

"A plain-spoken packet," said Shadrow, maliciously approving. "Full of fire and lyin' smiles. Never mind. You can't play double with me any more. Want to go away?"

"Yes," said the girl, so eagerly that Shadrow sat back in his chair and laughed.

"Well," he said, "you ain't gettin' the chance."

"Tade, there's a limit to this thing!"

"You bet," said the man. "We've just about come to it. Lynn, you're my ward and I've got to take care of you. It's settled. You'll marry me."

The girl straightened, and a long, wild flash of anger poured out of her eyes. "You're not frightening me, Tade!"

"Of course, not," said Shadrow, oddly quiet. "But the statement goes."

"Why, you——" breathed Lynn, and struggled for some adequate word. A deep, furious contempt swept over the expressive face. "So the cattle baron thinks to command a marriage, does he? The great Tade Shadrow! Listen. You are sixty years old, and there isn't a kind act in all those years to your credit. You're a coward and a bully; a cheat and a liar and a ruffian. There's not a soul in all this land that doesn't hate and despise you. All that you are worth you have stolen from weaker people. Perhaps you think yourself an iron character. Well, don't be deceived. You're cold enough to order a man killed—as you have ordered Hugh Tracy killed. But you hired it done, Tade. If you had to stand up and do your own fighting you'd squeal like a rat! I'd sooner marry a—a savage with filed teeth in the South Seas."

Shadrow took this verbal lashing in silence. His sagging features paled as the girl went on, and the burning brilliance of his eyes strengthened to raw flame. When she was through, he tried to beat down her glance with that infuriated stare—and failed. Suddenly he wrenched himself upright, one hand striking the table. He was breathing heavily, and the violent speech tumbled out of him. "Never mind—I'll show you who's master of this place! I'll break your back, girl! It was in my mind to make a kindly husband. It ain't so many years before I'll be dead. You'd have the property—to marry a younger and more pleasin' man if you chose! All right! I'll show you just how it feels to be hurt! You'll marry me and you'll never leave this ranch!"

"Force?" cried Lynn.

Shadrow's aged countenance filled with that malice always so near the surface. "There is no livin' man to contradict what I do, or to interfere. I am sendin' to town this afternoon for Judge Beakes and a license. He'll be here by supper time. You've got till then to think it over. If you can't see light, make up your mind to accept anything that might happen. That should be clear enough for you."

She stared incredulously at him, whispering: "I believe—I actually believe you'd do it."

"I can't force you to marry me in front of witnesses. But you'll be livin' here quite a while——"

She watched the petulant, womanish lips of this man press a grin into shapelessness. Then, turning away with a quick, pushing gesture, she walked out to the porch as if the air behind were too stifling to endure.

Meanwhile Maunders and Tolbert walked toward the grouped crew. The circle opened to let them in. A man in the center—one of the ranch guards—suddenly stopped talking and fell to scuffling up the dirt with a boot toe, but another said: "Tell Lake about this, Doby."

Doby looked at Tolbert. "I ain't got around to tellin' the boss yet. You better do it for me, Tolbert. There ain't any boys left down on Tracy's spur with the beef."

"What happened?" broke in Maunders.

Doby kept his eyes on Tolbert. "Well, Luke Gann came up from there night before last, right after all you fellows had gone after Tracy and the girl. Luke said the boys had just got squared around at Tracy's place when a couple of guns begin bangin' away from the top of the rim. It just raised hell. Nobody was hit, but the beef stampeded all over the desert. They tried to round up these jaspers, who just faded. Well, Luke said it was yes or no when the ball would start again from some other angle of the rim, and it was kind of discouragin'. Everybody decided it was too tough to be pot-shotted. So the bunch pulled stakes and hit for grass clean to the other side of nowhere. Luke said he was through, too. Nobody lookin' after the beef now."

Maunders turned on Tolbert. "There," he muttered, "is the beginnin' of the crack-up. I knew it would come. We've tried too hard to get Tracy—and we ain't got him. He's played it right—nibbled away at us."

"I don't mind sayin'," broke in Doby, "that I was in a hell of a sweat while you fellows was gone. Just three of us left behind to hold these quarters. We could've been burnt out easy enough."

"You can shake hands with yourself that you wasn't," grumbled Maunders.

"Yeah?" said Doby. "Well, I'm beginnin' to entertain a few doubts about this job. You fellows ever stop to think how many boys are smashed up on account of this ruction? And I'll tell you something else: TS is mighty unpopular. There's goin' to be a lot of lads belly-flat in the brush waitin' to drop a shot on any

Shadrow hand so foolish as to be ridin' solitary. It's kinda tough."

"For thirty dollars a month," said Maunders ironically, "you ought to be willin' to die."

"Yeah?" grunted Doby. "Yeah?"

That was the last talk for quite an interval. These men—there were better than forty in the circle—were studying their own fortunes with a scowling attention. Lake Tolbert looked coolly around, watching the dark faces crease up and show all the ranges of doubt and dissatisfaction. He knew them thoroughly. There was no loyalty in them, and little enough of goodness. A Shadrow hand was a picked hand. It took hard, unscrupulous men to stand the gaff. And now that their own skins were endangered, now that they felt the Shadrow power to be no longer unbreakable, they looked closely at their hole cards. Most of them, he realized, would bunch the job if it came to hard, even-matched fighting. What had so far held them was the tremendous power of Shadrow's reputation.

All this time his attention was half placed on the main house; and now he saw Lynn Isherwood come out of the door with a rapidity that meant trouble yonder. He saw her face to be pale, moved by agitation.

"What I want to know," said another hand, "is if Tracy figures he can come——"

Shadrow's yell sailed toward the group. "Tolbert—send me a man!"

The owner stood on the porch, clinging to one of the posts. Tolbert silently indicated a hand near by, who walked reluctantly over the plaza. The interrupted speaker went on: "—if Tracy figures he can come back?"

"You ain't seen the last of him," prophesied Maunders. "Damned right he'll be back. Look here. He had help up in that timber. A bunch of 'em, waiting for us to charge. And when he does come back he'll have more."

"He'll come here?"

Maunders slowly nodded, looking again at Tolbert. All the eyes of the group veered on this foreman who so far had said nothing. Tall and taciturn, a master of men, he swayed them through fear mostly, through respect to a lesser degree. It was his iron rule that had governed TS; the half-military discipline was of his making. And though there was no affection possible for such a man, these rough and unruly TS riders instinctively turned to him for judgment. It was long in coming. Locked still in his rigid calm, he watched the despatched hand come ambling

135

back from Shadrow. The fellow said slowly to the group: "I been sent to Antelope for Judge Beakes. He's to bring out a marriage license." Turning, he went for his horse.

"He must be gettin' childish," growled Maunders.

"Him and the girl?" grunted Doby and stared all around him. "Hell, she ain't doin' that by her own will."

"Never mind how it's done," warned somebody else. "It is none of your business, Doby."

"No skin off'n my nose," agreed Doby. "But it looks raw. Even to me it looks raw."

"Well," broke in another hand cynically, "she's old enough to know her book."

But Doby had another idea. "It's pretty rank, boys. And here's what will happen: it'll make a lot more people in the country want to wipe out Shadrow. If it is bad with us now, it'll be worse."

Tolbert pulled up his head. Instantly he got the full attention of the outfit. Into the waiting silence he dropped his sparing words one by one. It was a trick, a deliberate building up of suspense; and it heightened everything he said.

"Tracy will come back. He'll have help. You boys better think twice whether you want to get in another fight which will make any other fight look like a picnic."

"You're pullin' out?" demanded Doby.

"No," said Tolbert. "I'm stayin' for a spell longer. But don't let that influence you none. Think twice before you sleep here tonight."

That much curtly, flatly stated, he swung on his heels and walked away. Lynn Isherwood stood over at the throat of the plaza, staring down the Antelope road. The concealing shadows across his eyes again, he went toward her. She came slowly around and looked at him; and the man, never ceasing to pry into the faces and acts of others, saw somewhere in that glance a suppressed fear. Removing his hat, he halted before you.

"Shadrow asked to marry you, ma'am?"

"Yes," said the girl.

"You agreed?"

"No!"

"And so," went on Tolbert in that quietly relentless probing manner, "he said something about makin' you marry him?"

"Tolbert," parried the girl, "you are paid by Tade Shadrow. You work for him. You are no friend of mine. Why should I tell you?"

Tolbert's long, supple fingers slowly creased the edges of his hat. "I can readily see you trust me none."

"Why should I?"

He nodded slightly. "You're right. A man such as me knows nothing about women and never has a chance to learn—not about your kind of a woman. But it has been my observation that you judge on sort of first guess and seldom make a serious error."

"Well?" said Lynn, on the defensive.

"You made your judgment of me the first day you came to TS. You never changed that judgment. I am not askin' you to change it, for it was correct. I make no bones about it. Nor have I ever held a deceivin' opinion of my past or present life."

"Well?" repeated Lynn, uncertain and alarmed. There was always some purpose in this inexplicable man's mind and heart. There was one now, and she waited for it to come out with a species of dread.

"Yet," he went on, "I did you one favor you know about."

"Lied to Tade for me? Yes. I never understood it. Why did you?"

"I did you another favor which you don't know about. I led our crew off your trail and Tracy's trail as long as I could, hopin' for your escape."

"Why?" insisted the girl.

A rider loped into the plaza and dismounted at the porch, going directly to Shadrow's office. Heavy dust clouds folded and raveled through the motionless, burning air. Tolbert's eyes followed the rider as far as the office door, watchful and reflective. Afterwards he turned back to Lynn.

"I seldom explain," he said. "A man's acts should speak for him—and always do. My life has been a hard life, ma'am, and worth nobody's sympathy. I was early taught to give no favors and to ask none. I never have."

"Which is brutal," interrupted Lynn.

He inclined his head slowly. "Perhaps. Still, there is no mercy in the kind of men you see in this plaza. They are old enough to know what they're doing. With them it's dog eat dog. It's been so with me. The strong dog lives and the weak one dies. I am alive. That's the sum of the proposition. You can't go behind it. In order to live I've been as fast as the fastest, hard as the hardest. I expected I always would be that way. The favor I did you was about the first I ever did for anybody."

"But why?" repeated the girl.

Shadrow was yelling from his office: "Maunders—Maunders, come here!" And once again Tolbert's glance pinned itself to the doorway and remained there until Maunders went rolling in. Looking again at the girl, he seemed to find the right words with difficulty: "The worst man in the world has got some deadline. Otherwise, he'd have no pride. And a man without pride is a dog. Never mind what I've done. Some things I never did. I don't ask you to believe me, and there's no reason why you should. But, ma'am, I never ruined a woman. Nor will I let any other man. I shall be on this ranch till Tracy comes back."

"You——"

Shadrow was calling again, more angrily: "Tolbert, I want you!"

The foreman bowed stiffly at Lynn. "Tracy will show up," he muttered and climbed to the porch. Cruising along it with an exaggerated deliberateness, he halted at the doorway and swayed slightly forward. Shadrow stood visible against a wall; Maunders was somewhere beyond sight. Ducking his head beneath the doorway's top member, Tolbert entered, instantly seeking out Maunders, who had stationed himself in a far corner. Tolbert paused, watchfully placed between these two.

"Lake," grunted Shadrow, full of suppressed fury, "you've played me double!"

Tolbert's attention was on Maunders now, and he said with a quiet sibilance: "Come a little forward, Sid. I don't want you over there."

Maunders's face was at once aroused and attentive. Saying nothing, he walked on until he no longer covered the foreman's left flank.

"A mighty careful man!" observed Shadrow. "A mighty careful man, Mister Tolbert!"

Tolbert's inscrutable eyes clung to Shadrow. "What is it to be, Tade?"

"A rider," said Tade, between his teeth, "just found Bat Testervis dead up along the trail."

"You ought to be glad of it."

"Should hey? Looky here, Lake. You came back to meet me yesterday mornin' from that trail. You said there wasn't anything over that way. You lied. Bat was over that way. The shot I heard was your shot. You dropped him and said nothing of it to me."

Tolbert held his tongue, glance reverting to Maunders. Increasing strain showed on the burly gunman's broad and blunt visage; in the smoky slate eyes centered on Tolbert was a broadening light.

"Deny it?" snapped Shadrow, impatient of the lagging silence.

"No," said Tolbert.

"Open up—open up!" yelled Shadrow. "You've got something to explain here and now!"

"Nothing," denied Tolbert. "I never explain. Make out your own ticket."

It plainly astonished Shadrow. Starting forward from the wall, he reached his desk and supported himself on it with the flats of his hands, half crouched in the position, and his overgrown head tipped oddly on the skinny neck. "I have had," said he, more composedly, "about enough of your ingrown, pussyfoot ways. No man grinds his own coffee in my mill, Lake. No man, ever. You may think you're big enough to buck me, but you ain't. Before your time foremen have made that fatal mistake. Now you open up!"

Tolbert never moved, never relaxed the pressure of his thin lips. It was Maunders who broke in speaking to Tolbert as if Shadrow didn't exist. "I get this now," said the heavy-set gunman. "I make you now, Lake. It's that girl you're lookin' after. By God, that's the game you been playin' all the time. And you tried to tell me you wasn't playin' any game."

Shadrow rapped out: "What's between you two mugs?"

Maunders went on, brushing aside the owner's question. Clearly he was holding a tight bridle on himself. "And that sort of clears up your kindly advice to me when I went for Tracy that night at his cabin. I was to bust right in and not delay, was I? You knew right then the girl was on her way to tell Tracy he'd be visited. And you wanted me to get my vest punctured. Good boy, Lake! You figure fast."

"You men," said Shadrow, "better go outside and settle if there's blood between you."

Maunders threw himself about as if he meant to charge Shadrow. "That's what you want, ain't it? Damn you, Shadrow, you've put your dirty chores on me long enough! I'll do no more. Right now Hugh Tracy's prowlin' for me, and there ain't room enough in all the Powder for the both of us to live! Who started that? You did, you fox-faced, shysterin', belly-crawlin' digger! Well, from this point on you'll be shy one rider. I'm gone. I've got a chore to do. If I do it, I'll stay in this country—and you can be damned well sure I'll take my commission out of you!"

He swung for the door, smoldering. On the threshold he pulled himself around and stared at Tolbert. "It's all right, Lake. You and me been playin' this scoundrel's game too long, and I ain't holdin' the trick against you. You better clear out before he ribs you another way."

Tolbert listened to the big man's boots scuff across the porch

139

and strike the packed dirt of the plaza. But even as he listened, he watched Shadrow's wolf-shrewd face betray the presence of another thought. He had read this man's changing moods for years, and now, detecting that feral expression, he recognized in it a meaning for him. Not so many days ago it had been on Shadrow's face when the owner had issued Willy Bones's death warrant.

Shadrow said abruptly: "Quit starin' at me, Lake. And you're through. Roll up your war bag and light out."

"No," said Tolbert. "I'm stayin'."

"Lake," said Shadrow, and suddenly sat down in his chair— "Lake, get out of my office."

The foreman's cheeks had been unchangingly set for too many years to break out of the habitual mask now. But there was in his eyes that faint light of contempt as he stared at the older man. "Don't telegraph your desire so plain, Tade. You want to kill me, sure. I always knew that would be the way of it when we split up. I know too much about your business to get away free. But your house is crumblin'. Roof and wall, it's crumblin'. And I'll stick awhile to see it fall!"

He went through the door with a sudden alert twist of his body and stepped aside. He heard Shadrow rise and run across the floor, he heard the office door slam shut behind. Dropping to the yard, he went deliberately along the line of buildings that closed the western edge of the plaza. Ahead of him the crew still formed a circle by the bunkhouse. And toward the crew he walked, taking his roundabout way that placed the tool shed and the blacksmith shop on his immediate flank.

Sid Maunders came out of a bunkhouse and went through the gathered hands, saying something. He came past the men and struck over toward the small barn, two hundred feet opposite Tolbert. Reaching it, he went inside. Tolbert kept his stride, arrived at the open arch of the blacksmith shop—and whirled into it with a rapid, gliding twist of his body. Somebody in the crowd shouted, "Watch out!" The sultry air of the compound was smashed asunder by the full-throated roar of a gun. Daylight appeared in a board beside Tolbert, who stood unmoved, arms idle. Maunders cried out from the small barn:

"Come on, Lake! I'm here waitin' for you!"

"I'm not drawin'," called Tolbert, emotionlessly.

"Come on!" raged Maunders.

"Not today, Sid. There's bigger fish in the ocean than suckers."

"Tolbert!" shouted the hidden gunman. "Tolbert, I'll step out of here shootin' if you will!"

140

"You dumb ox," said Tolbert, "get on a horse and go before you're hurt."

A long silence followed, and the oppressive heat seemed to increase throughout the dreary yard. The TS riders stood motionless by the bunkhouses, swarthy faces glistening under the slanting rays of the sun; and in one cool, detached survey Lake Tolbert saw the bold avidness for a killing as plain as the written word on them. Nowhere was a sign of pity, of generosity. Yet this lack had on him no effect, for these were qualities he little understood and never had expected. Maunders shouted again, meaninglessly; and directly thereafter the big gunman spurred out of the end of the small barn and raced down the Antelope road.

It was like the break of a long-held vacuum. Air and sound rushed in. Stepping out of the bunkhouse, Tolbert saw the crew swirl into groups and these groups collect into definite parties. There were two such parties, one drifting for the bunkhouses while the other held fast. Tolbert knew then what it was to be. The first party presently came out with war bags packed to go, and in compact formation marched over to the tethered horses. All these man swung to the saddle and wheeled in front of Shadrow's office.

"Shadrow."

Shadrow never appeared. A coyote howl rose up from the seated men. Somebody fired once to the sky, and then in unison the dissenters wheeled and charged down the road. A long cloud of dust obscured them. Tolbert slowly reached for his cigarette papers and turned to face the remaining group. There—twenty-some hands out of all that young army once Shadrow's—were left to fight; and these were the oldest in point of service on the ranch, dating beyond his own tenure. Watching that sullen, silent cluster, Tolbert understood that from this moment on he had no authority over them. These men stayed because of the ranch itself, because of the threatened fight in the offing, or because of some obscure loyalty or pride they themselves knew little about. But they would answer to Shadrow, not to him. More exactly—and Tolbert's narrow inspection hardened as he decided it—he was no longer one of them. They regarded him with a covert hostility. The old discipline had fallen, he himself was now an alien on this ranch he had ruled for so long; he was amongst enemies—quite alone. Standing there in this strange new isolation, it came to him that he should have killed Maunders, who would never quit the Powder without finding and settling with Hugh Tracy. And it came to him also that for the first time

141

in his hard, unforgiving career he was violating the first article of his faith—he was forgetting his own safety in the effort to protect another human being. Over the trailing cigarette smoke he observed audibly: "I must be gettin' along in years. I must be gettin' old."

When the cook's triangle clanged out the belated dinner signal, he walked to the dining room and took his accustomed place with an iron impassivity that locked the rest of the world away from his aloof and lonely thoughts.

CHAPTER 14

JERKED DOWN

"It's risky," reflected Bill Vivian.

"Sure," agreed Hugh and drank the coffee pot dry. An overhead sun bombed the glade with one blazing shaft and another, destroying the last bit of forest cool; all the surrounding greenery had lost its dew-coated brilliance and was now a dully dusted jade. Cross-legged on the earth, the heaviness of sleep not yet worn off, Hugh watched the gravely attentive faces around him. It was exaclty half-past one by his watch. "What in thunder did you let me snooze so long for?" he grumbled.

"You needed it," stated Bill.

"The morning's lost."

"What of it? Trouble won't spoil for a little keepin'. Well, it's risky. They's just the twelve of us."

"I'll go ahead alone."

Bill Vivian gave his partner a severe glance. "The hell you will. We stick together."

"I'm putting it up to you boys," said Hugh. "I am through running. I'm turning the other direction. But it doesn't obligate a single one of you to come along."

Bill swelled visibly and turned toward the others with an ironic regard. "Listen to him. Why, you cockeyed horse thief, what did I get these mugs for?"

Hugh grinned. "Well, then, quit stalling."

"I only said we could lay over another day and drag these hills. I can find half a dozen more lads itchin' to be in the future developments."

"Day's too much," contradicted Hugh. "Bill, I'm about finished with caution. It always leads me astray. The time to do a thing is when you feel it can be done."

"Yeah," drawled Bill, "I've heard that song before. Enough times to say it in my sleep. Keep hittin' until somethin' drops. Press your luck while it lasts. Never mind the consequences. I know. Same tune sung by the same big bass voice of Hugh Tracy, Esquire. Go on, tell me something new."

"If we wait," added Hugh imperturbably, "we give Shadrow that much time to get organized. Meanwhile, we're on the outside looking in. We're too far away. No, it won't do."

"What's to be gained by going to Antelope?"

Tracy leaned forward, stabbing his finger at Bill. "Twelve men can hold Antelope against a regiment of cavalry, my boy. It's Shadrow's town. He needs it. He gets his supplies from there and he transacts his business from there. We'll ease in, seal Antelope up, and wait. Sooner or later he'll get aggravated enough to make a move against us. After that——" and Hugh spread his palms upward.

"A thought," said Bill reluctantly. "Only, if he ever put a ring of guns around Antelope and settled down to one of these all-summer affairs——"

"We're inside, he's out," suggested Hugh. "You can't starve a man who's using a grocery store as a fort."

Suddenly Bill slapped his knee, and the homely visage cracked wide open with a grin. "Somehow it sort of looks like a dirty joke on Shadrow. Good! I'm for it."

"Willy," said one of the others, "is coming across the flat."

"But supposin' he lets us strictly alone," pondered Bill. "Then we're in a town and what of it?"

"He won't," said Hugh quickly. "I won't let him."

"I thought so. You've got another idea in your noggin. Don't hold out on me, mister."

"The rest is my personal affair."

"More ridin' off alone, huh? You might as well make up your mind I'll be along."

Willy Bones spurred into the glade, a crust of sweat on his horse. But he dismounted casually and reached for his cigarettes before speaking.

"I'm right on top of the rim above Antelope. Shadrow ain't over there"—waving his hand toward the canyon country—"any more. I find him on the road home. This is three hours ago."

"What's it look like in Antelope?"

"Which is why I come back," said Willy and paused to crimp and light his smoke. Bill Vivian said impatiently:

"Yeah, I know you're one of these big, strong-handed fellows with a close mouth. You've made it clear. Now go on."

"Pretty close to twenty-twenty-five hands ride down the rim road from TS and pile into Antelope."

"Shadrow's hands?"

"I don't make out. But who else would they be?"

"That's right," agreed Hugh. "Foolish question, Bill."

"This cub," grumbled Bill, "has been eatin' too much raw meat."

Willy flushed and grew embarrassed beneath the concerted scrutiny of all those older eyes. 'Well," he said uncertainly, "I ain't tryin' to throw my weight about. I only mean——"

"Stick to your guns, Willy," drawled Hugh. "You're head high to anybody in this company, not exceptin' a shriveled little weasel named Vivian. Go on. They went into Antelope."

"Yeah. And out again. They don't stop for more'n a drink. I see 'em go right straight across Powder, towards the long hill up Dead Axle grade."

"Then," cried Bill Vivian, "they're through with Shadrow! They're jumpin' herd! I told you TS was bustin' up."

"Wait a minute," interposed one of the other men. "It may be Shadrow's sent 'em out to circle these parts. Don't be too previous."

But Hugh, rising to his feet, slowly shook his head. "No, Bill's got the answer. That bunch is leaving Powder. Times are gettin' a little tough, and the thirty dollars and board won't hold a fellow who's wondering about his own skin. We've shook some of the strength out of TS."

"Lessee," murmured Vivian. "You said twenty-five, Willy? I'd judge Shadrow had that many or more left. He's already lost or fired most of the outlyin' crews. But make no mistake about it—those remainin' on the premises represent the boilin' of a tough mess."

A long halloo struck out of the trees, and presently Sabe Venner, rolling his big body low in the saddle to avoid being brushed by the branches, came into the clearing. "I tell you——" he began.

Bill Vivian interrupted him smoothly: "The TS boys passed you. Up Dead Axle grade."

Sabe Venner stared. "Who's tellin' this story, you or me?"

"Which way did they go?"

"Straight on with the road. Looked to me 'sif it was a case of long dust and no stops. I made a high peak and got a last sight of them just a little while back. They was clear over on the Burnt Creek ridge."

A silence came to the group. Hugh Tracy stared out upon the flats with a shadowed thoughtfulness, and his eyes ran all along the far edge of timber. Bill Vivian, never able to be entirely still, rocked on his heels and watched Tracy until the monotony of it oppressed his nerves. "Well," he said finally, "grass won't grow if you stand on it."

"We'll go across the flat and hit a course for Antelope."

"Might be somebody planted yonder waitin' for a good shot."

But Tracy walked back to his horse and mounted. "No, don't think so now. This part of the game is all played out. If Shadrow's having trouble with his men he won't scatter them. He'll draw everything back to the ranch."

"We're talked dry," said Vivian. "Let's do something for a change."

Tracy led the group out of the glade and down the slope to the trail. Turning into the desert, he struck straight across. Bill Vivian forged abreast; the others, taking a cue from the recent skirmish, deployed and presented a broad front. "Better avoid that canyon," advised Bill, and his pale green eyes went skipping along the line of timber ahead. Willy Bones drew his gun and held it in his lap.

But there was no question. Tracy reached the rocky margin of timber, passed by swinging arcs up the broken incline, and attained the beginning of the canyon trail. A little farther on he left it abruptly and headed toward the right. Over there the terrain swelled and hollowed away like a rolling sea, gulch and ridge alternating in endless succession. For a brief while Hugh had a good view of it as it swept higher into the peaks of the middle Mogul reaches; then, descending into the half-light and the long solitude of the great pines, he lost the horizon altogether. Trail ran into trail each small and vague; following these at an easy pace, he kept bearing off to the eastward. In that direction the general rim of the plateau reared itself from the desert. Single-file, the other men came silently behind. But presently Bill Vivian, directly to the rear of Hugh, began a casual talk:

"You know, Hugh, there's more women in the world than men."

"What of it?" grunted Hugh.

"Maybe," reflected Bill, "that's why there's so much trouble. One of these days I think I'll take a vacation and follow that idea to some sort of a conclusion."

"Don't use your head for something it wasn't built to stand."

Bill's chuckle was softly infectious. "Remember the night in Antelope when Sam Lafferty's boys figured you for an easy mark? It was a swell-lookin' barroom when we got through with it." And after a short spell of quiet he added wistfully: "Wonder if there'll ever be any old times like that again?"

"Don't look backward," said Hugh . "Don't ever make that mistake. Look ahead. For what it's worth, which is little, and for what you can see, which is almost nothing, look ahead. If you start sorting out the relics of the past, you blamed fool, you'll get nothing but a headache."

"Still," insisted Bill, "we used to have a wallopin' good time."

"Sure. Too young to know any better. We figured there wasn't any day but the one in hand. We never had a dime, never worried, never cared. It's only when a man gets ambitious and begins to lay up possessions that he runs into grief."

"Moral—don't get ambitious."

"A fine moral," growled Hugh, "for vegetables."

That exasperated Bill, who made nothing of these sudden contradictions of his partner. "Well, what in thunder is it all about then?"

"There is no answer," said Hugh, with a return of the old rebellious bitternesss. Then directly afterwards he added: "But if a man was meant for anything, I guess it is to keep ramming ahead till he finds something that will do for an answer."

"Sort of a joke on him then," observed Bill shrewdly, "if he reaches the end of his picket rope and don't find none."

"Well, he's anyhow put in the time trying. That's probably as good as the answer itself."

Bill vented a disgusted, horsy snort. "What the hell are we mumbling about? This palaver goes around in circles like a dog reachin' for its tail. Yeah, I've heard it before from you and it don't mean a thing. You talk one way, then you talk another. It's yes and then it's no. You make wild passes about nothing bein' worth nothin' and I get to thinkin' you're slippin'. Then you go out and smack down six hands and the cook and I say to myself, 'Here's old Hughey back home again.' Sometimes you just defeat me. Your old thinker don't track with your muscles at all. To hear you say so, we're licked before we start and there ain't no use startin'. But I have lived with you goin' on twelve years, and I never saw you delay startin' anything you wanted to start, regardless of how you figured it would turn out."

"Pass the plate, parson," drawled Hugh, "and I'll give you a lead nickel."

"Anyhow," grumbled Bill, "I miss the old neighborly brawls we don't have no more."

That was all. Once again they reached a clear crest and sighted Mogul's slanting slopes and broken tiers; descending immediately afterwards to the forest, they went steadily on while the twilight grew heavy with lavender and the golden bars of the late sun broke more infrequently through the matted branch tops. Dusk came to them twice. It came softly to them here; half an hour later Hugh made a sharp swing rightward, rode to the very margin of Mogul's rim and saw dusk falling again, over the prairie in rolling purple waves. The lights of Antelope lay below, winking up with a fractured brilliance.

"I'll go down and scout," murmured Hugh. "If it looks all right I'll come right back."

"No," objected Bill. "We got in a jackpot once before doing this split act."

"The trouble last time," said Hugh, pointedly, "was that you couldn't hold your fiddlin' feet in one place. Try to curb that herd-jumpin' instinct for once."

"Rats!" grumbled Bill.

"A crushing reply," gibed Hugh and went forward. Within a dozen paces the pony's head and shoulders dropped down a severe grade that had the vague appearance of being blasted from the sheer wall. It descended in one long, unbroken pitch—a mere ledge without wagon width at any point. When he reached the bottom, Antelope was the farther away by a good three quarters of a mile. Swinging back, he put the pony to a gentle rack and gradually drew toward the southern end of the town.

This was the brighter side; the last building against the desert was the courthouse, whose dimmed lights crossed the street mouth and made a kind of hurdle for him to pass. Curling off, he halted at a point from which he could survey the walks. There was, as far as he could make out, little life tonight in this Antelope that ran the extreme of flood and ebb. A cowbell tinkled, a hammer fell, one man's talk drifted on into the darkness. That was about all. He discovered but three horses standing at the racks, these in front of Lou Burkey's saloon. Nobody appeared on the street.

But the barrier of light troubled him, and so he cut a circle into the desert and passed around the town, to arrive at the northern margin where the line of poplars condensed the quality of the dark and precipitated it toward the earth in a ghostly rain. Dust smell clung strongly to the air, the mark of a recent traveler. But all the near half of town was lightless, and utilizing this advantage he passed in between the silhouetted building fronts at a casual walk. One man's cigarette tip glowed and died and glowed again in the runway of the stable—Jinks Bailey's stable. Behind the man was an ineffectual plaque of dimmed lantern light. Hugh veered toward the runway, head tilted down until the sweep of his hat concealed his face.

"Evenin'."

"Evenin'," said the other slowly.

"Jinks?"

"Me."

"How's things?"

"Oh, so-so," said Jinks Bailey and lowered his cigarette. His body shifted in casual deliberateness. "I can't see you. Who is it?"

"Where's everybody?"

Bailey let out a small grunt. "If you don't know that you musta come out of a deep grave."

"Nobody much in town?"

"No-o."

Hugh pressed the pony on into the stable, rode the length of the runway and back again.

"What's that for?" challenged Bailey.

"Curiosity," said Hugh and angled across the street to Burkey's high porch. He left the horse and stepped toward the swinging doors. Against them, he changed his mind and moved on to the window. Through this dull, dust-grained surface he saw Burkey fairly definitely. Two other men, unrecognizable, sat farther back in the room. Once more coming to the doors, he pushed them open sufficiently to have some prior knowledge of what he stepped into, and then walked through. The men in the rear of the place were known to him by little more than name—being oldish hands who had prospected the hills. Reassured, he laid his attention on Burkey.

The saloonman's palms lifted slowly and fell flat on the bar, and across his noncommittal face streaked a momentary astonishment. Knowing there was no greeting called for, Hugh offered none. Peremptorily, he asked:

"Anybody in town, Lou?"

Burkey shook his head with a slow, exaggerated side-to-side gesture. There was a show of brilliance in the black eyes—a quick and uncontrolled brilliance that evaded the otherwise studied gravity. Seeing it, Hugh spoke again: "Nobody that I should know—or shouldn't know, Lou?"

Burkey's lips compressed as his head moved once more in denial. Reaching beneath the counter, he brought up a piece of cloth and began casually to mop a bar that needed no mopping. The gesture was innocent, but it brought Tracy's eyes directly down to that bar's shining surface, and he noticed for the first time a filled whisky glass sitting there and a cigar beside it. From the tip of that cigar, half consumed, a faint spiral of smoke curled. Lou Burkey stared past Tracy to one of the old fellows.

149

"Sam, step up and finish your drink and take your stogy off here before it burns a hole in the counter."

There was something wrong here. Tracy wheeled about and watched the indicated Sam rise in reluctance and advance. The man drooped his closed fist into a coat pocket with a gesture of uncertainty. Tracy's prying glance caught the stem of a pipe projecting from that fist. Yet he maintained his outward manner of calm and turned back to Burkey.

"I won't disturb you by askin' for a drink," he said briefly and turned to go out. Alert, strongly warned, he kicked the doors wide before him and slid through. A long sidewise pace put him away from the reflected lights, flat against the saloon wall. Stationed there, all his nerves went cold and tight. One of those three horses standing by the porch was Tade Shadrow's solid sorrel, recognizable anywhere along the Powder. Next moment he hurried on, reached the porch end, and dropped into the solid dark thereabouts. Sharply reviewing the stable, he saw nothing of Jinks Bailey's cigarette glow; but farther down the street, toward the poplars, a body moved from walk to walk with a cat-footed swiftness.

Hugh thought rapidly: "Shadrow wouldn't be here without his men. So it's somebody else riding Shadrow's horse. It wouldn't be Lynn. It's either Tolbert or Maunders. Whichever one, he went out the back way of Burkey's leaving that whisky and cigar." Then, all his faculties whetted by this threat stalking the dripping black, he went on with his reasoning, each thought framed in his mind as clear and brief and swift as talk: "I never saw Tolbert smoke a cigar. So it's Maunders. He went out the back way of the saloon. That was him crossing to the east side. He'll be trying for a fair shot."

Retreating from the porch end, he paused on the balls of his feet, momentarily uncertain. Some faint thread of sound straggled out of that area behind the stable—to make his decision for him. He passed along the side wall of Burkey's building, reached the abysmal gloom of its rear, and groped between back porches and rubbish piles until he arrived at the alley separating the general store and the saddle shop. This he took, drifting forward to the street again. The stable was almost directly opposite. Watching its runway, he saw Jinks Bailey's lantern go out.

"He won't be running," thought Hugh, mind on Sid Maunders. "He's tried for me too long. He's too stubborn to quit. Why didn't he make his stand in the saloon?"

It was odd enough. Yet this was a game of blood, motivated by surreptitious and fragmentary impulses, in which man reverted to animal cunning. Logic had nothing to do with it; there was never much logic in the mind of one about to kill or be killed. A faint rattle emerged from the stable and died, and Hugh wondered if Bailey, the turncoat Bailey, had a part in this. The thought brought along a small heat of anger, the only personal emotion he felt. Toward Maunders he now experienced none of the fulminating rage of past times. The episode had gone too far; it had begun so long ago that at present it was in the nature of an inevitable happening, advancing move by move, as certain as the stars above. It was a fixed condition of his life and of Maunders's life—the burning man-to-man animosities quite gone. Impersonally reviewing that sentiment so utterly dominating him, he saw himself and the big gunman propelled willy-nilly by the fiat of those indifferent gods who ruled. And standing there, his pulse slow and steady, his head clear as a bell, bereft of nerves, he caught the quick tapping of footfalls on his left—down by the town's dark end again. Maunders had passed back to this side of the street.

"He's trying to place me against the courthouse lights," decided Hugh and ran softly over the dust to the stable. Between the stable and the adjoining rooming house he swung and made his stand, having parried Maunders's move and once more put the gunman opposite. Time dragged out. An indistinct rasping echo floated from the stable runway, and a bit of glow fell out of it, to die the next moment. Bailey was signaling.

Maunders's bulky body struck something over behind the saddle shop. The minor report of that collision made an actual reverberation in the singing stillness; and as if it were the break in a tension impossible to hold longer, other things immediately came to Hugh's ears. Above him, directly above him, a second-story window of the rooming house grated against a tight casing; up there a man whispered hoarsely. Straining the import of it through that exceedingly fine mesh of suspicion, he tossed the rumor aside. It was, he believed, some spectator more agitated than himself. Water dripped melodiously out of the stable trough, and through the stable wall seeped the patient stamp of stalled ponies and the rub of their halters against the feed boxes. There was a suspiration of an easy night wind through the poplars over by the graveyard. A deep voice—Maunders's lowering, breath-clotted voice—said:

"Come out, Tracy."

The maneuvering was over. Maunders had weakened and turned reckless.

Rigid along the wall, Tracy raked the dense shadow whence

151

the challenge had come. He studied all those shadows opposite as far as the saloon, saw nothing. Maunders said again, "Come out, Tracy," with a terrific calm—and Hugh's attention fell upon the man's dim bulk lodged at the near corner of the saloon, aside the street glow. Tracy estimated that distance at ninety feet. He thought of Jinks Bailey and of the man whispering above—and then he closed his mind to thinking. Walking forward from the alley, he passed beyond the sidewalk and halted in the street.

"All right, Sid."

Hugh saw the man swing about, and he knew then Maunders had expected him to be in the other direction—over by the courthouse and against those lights. Maunders's breath poured out in heavily expelled gusts. "Tracy," he cried, "I could of run but I didn't! This has gone on too long! I'm goin' to find out about that cursed luck of yours now and here! One of us don't ride any more!"

"Go ahead, Sid," called out Tracy. His fist came from behind at a sweep, touched the gun butt and carried it up. Maunders was moving, but the man's great bulk cast a denser shadow because of that movement, and on the spreading outline Tracy pinned a still, deliberate muzzle. One rushing, exploding crack of sound overwhelmed Antelope's dark street and raced away in spinning, lesser fragments. Behind Tracy a board set up a screeching protest as the spent bullet struck. That was Maunders, speaking first. Tracy's own gun kicked back, and all the furious reverberations beat up afresh. Powder smoke drifted into his face. Maunders came strangely out of his position, staggering across the walk into the light. He was hit, but his gun rose again, and Tracy, pressing his will doggedly and brutally into the shot, fired once more on the fairer target. Maunders's head rolled back, then it tipped down—raggedly down—and all his joints buckled. He fell soundless and died without moving.

Tracy said, droning out the words: "Bailey, you bet on the wrong horse. Come away from the stable."

Bailey's voice traveled sullenly through the deep and dismal quiet: "I had nothing to do with this, Hugh."

"Come out," commanded Tracy. "I want to see you."

The saloon doors swung. Lou Burkey stood framed in the light, saying nothing at all. A man ran from the courthouse, calling: "What's happened? Who's that—who's down?" There was a rattling of windows from the darkened houses all along the street. Tracy's talk hit Lou Burkey like the curling end of a whip.

"I knew you in better days, Lou, and considered you had some grain. Shadrow's made putty out of you. If you couldn't be for me, why couldn't you keep your damned hand off me?"

"I never made a move your way, now or at any time."

"You lie, the same as Jinks Bailey lies. That glass and cigar belonged to Sid. He went out your back door when I came in. You tried to cover him."

The saloonman's voice broke a little. "Damn you, Hugh! You ain't the one that lives with the fear of God hangin' over your head day and night!"

"No?" said Hugh, coolly. "No?"

"No!" shouted Burkey. "And you've done nothing to help us by killin' Sid Maunders! It's us in Antelope that will get all hell hazed out of us when you're gone!"

"Maybe——" began Hugh and stopped. Bill Vivian and the other men drove into Antelope's street with a rush and a yell. Vivian lifted an arresting arm, brought his pony to a grinding halt, and shouted at the shadows: "Hugh!"

"Never mind," said Hugh quietly. "I didn't take the bullet, Bill."

"Who was it?"

"Maunders. He's dead. But nobody can accuse him of not tryin'." And a contemptuous anger stained his words. "The man was a scoundrel, a rascal and a trickster. But he never hid behind small words. He had guts. That's for your informatiion, Burkey, and it goes for the lick-spittle gentlemen of this town that crossed their fingers and prayed for the profits to continue. There is no place in hell deep enough or hot enough for a man that swallows his pride and plays a game he don't believe in."

"Fine—fine!" said Burkey and clipped the words between his teeth. "You're drunk with luck, but the jag won't last. Shadrow runs this country and will continue to do so. You're through. And the gentlemen of Antelope will play the winning side, as it is their right to do."

"Hughey," said Bill Vivian with a false gentleness, "he's speaking out of turn. Shall I belt him?"

"You're through!" yelled Burkey, losing his head. "And here's something that will put you back a notch! Judge Beakes left for TS this afternoon with a marryin' license. If it's the girl you're putting on the entertainment for, never mind. She'll be tied to Shadrow by now!"

Hugh Tracy sprang across the porch and caught the saloonman at the neck. "If you're lying to me, Lou, I'll break your back!"

Burkey strangled out a curse. "You wild fool! I have waited a long time to see some of the pride knocked out of your bully head! She's married now! Pull off your hands or I'll kill you!''

Hugh Tracy's mind went dim. He lifted Burkey and shook him like a loose sack. He whirled the man about and threw him out to the street; and then he ran to the pony racked at the porch. In the saddle, he shouted madly at the waiting riders: ''Come on—or stay behind!'' And his roweling spurs fell deep into the pony's flanks, sending it off down the street in great lunges. Bill Vivian emitted a rebel shout and leaned low in the saddle, pursuing. The whole line stretched out, beating through the dark, leaving a high curtain of dust behind, leaving Lou Burkey in the street to spit out his rage. One high call came back to Antelope—Bill Vivian sounding his shrill, eerie war cry at the bright and eternal stars.

CHAPTER 15

END AND BEGINNING

HUGH raced on past the poplars and down the desert road overshadowed by the scowling face of Mogul. Fury rioted in his head, and only one clear thought rose through it—the thought that he must reach and destroy Shadrow. Rather, it was not a thought, but an enraged, furnance-hot desire. Such sane impulses as he had brought to Antelope town this night were gone—swept up in the smoke of consuming temper. All the considered plans were so much ruin. There could not now be any waiting, and planning. Nothing was left but to smash ahead—destroy. Moved by this conviction, he hurled his body into the labored run of the horse, timing himself to the forward surges, bending far aside as the beast rounded curves.

"She played into his hands," he told himself, and wondered why the passing moments went so swiftly and the dim miles were so long. It was a bitter fact—Lynn had played into Tade Shadrow's hands. Now reviewing what had gone before, he wished he had taken the time to explain to the girl Shadrow's intrinsic character. With that knowledge, she never would have returned to Shadrow—no matter how desperate their situation might have seemed on the bald-topped butte. It was starkly clear to him. Shadrow certainly knew by now what his, Hugh's, feelings for the girl were. And balked in his one long-sought act of vengefulness, he would turn to this other piece of mad devil-try with an increased stubbornness, understanding surely that nothing could so hurt, so irretrievably wreck.

"It's the same thing," said Hugh, aloud to the night, "he's done all his life." No man knew what amount of pure ruin lay behind Shadrow, how much there was of grim and conscience-less injustice in that cruel career. When Shadrow was done with a victim nothing remained but misery. "By God, I'll see he never strikes again!"

Judge Beakes, so Burkey had said, had gone on to TS in the afternoon—another crawling, double-faced henchman who would obey Shadrow implicitly. It was utterly inconceivable that Lynn would give her consent to the marriage. Yet that made little difference. The marriage would be performed and its illegality would never be published. Or if the marriage were not made this day, Shadrow would use the brutal power in his hands to break Lynn's spirit. Hugh Tracy had no need to enlarge the thought. It was as bald and blunt as all the rest of Shadrow's tactics. Nor was there any hope of a softer treatment.

For as he rode, he knew Shadrow would carry out such a plan without compunction or scruple. There was actually no chance of a last-moment relenting. Not from Shadrow. This cattleman whose desires had never known a curb would force the girl, one way or another, into the ceremony—and make it valid by the threat of his power. Somewhere in the TS owner's make-up was a streak of primitive violence, a savagery that considered no law.

The TS side road was invisible in the dark, but Hugh knew the district too well to grope for it. At the same unchecked speed, he veered, hit the incline, and let the pony have its own way about going up. At the top the beast was deeply drawing, needing a blow; the rest of the boys were quite a distance behind. But he could not stop, and so he forged northward over the flat heights.

Bill Vivian meanwhile had made the effort to draw abreast; but the effort took too much out of his pony. So he contented himself with keeping the pace. At the side road he called ahead and got no answer. Reaching the summit, he called again and only saw Hugh dimly beating away. Knowing Hugh as well as he did, a deep apprehension overtook him, and he checked in until the rest of the outfit drew abreast.

"Sabe!"

"Yeah," said the young giant, cutting out of the line.

"That fool won't listen to anything!" bawled Bill. "He'll walk right in! I don't know what we're up against, but you and me have got to keep by him! Makes no difference what happens— we've got to keep right by him!"

"Better ketch him first," grunted Sabe Venner.

They took the road side by side, quirts snapping down; and by degrees they drew clear of the others. Yet twenty minutes later, when the first TS light winked through the night, they had not overtaken Hugh. Bill Vivian began to swear. "They'll pick us up sure as little green apples——"

He hauled back violently. Hugh said curtly: "Slow down. We'll walk the next half-mile."

"I thought you'd gone clean out of your noodle," growled Bill Vivian. "And still think so."

"At a walk," warned Hugh. The rest of the group piled up

and spilled out of the road. Hugh went on, overreaching his own admonition and traveling at a light canter. That single light ahead brightened; dimmer lights began to stud the horizon. And they were suddenly startled by the echo of a single shot rushing out of the TS compound.

"Now who's quarrelin'?" muttered Bill.

Hard on his phrase followed a short burst of firing, a concerted explosion of three or four guns, the sound rolling deeper into the night. Hugh said something indistinctly. The shadowed outline of all the TS buildings broke through the pall; silence settled inside the plaza.

Hugh stopped, stepped to the ground, whispering:

"Follow behind."

He advanced at a dogtrot, pitched into an arroyo, rose from it. Bill Vivian, right at his elbow, put in a quick warning: "Careful— careful! Something's up."

Hugh paused while the others spread abreast. Directly ahead was the bulk of the little barn, to the left of it a corner of the main house. The road ran between, into the plaza; and from this point of view they could see the bunkhouses aglow and men hurrying back and forth across the open without much order. Hugh whispered rapidly:

"You boys crawl along the small barn and flank those bunkhouses. The crew's all over there. I'm going to the back of the big house and look in."

He advanced immediately at a cat-footed run, Bill Vivian shadowing him all the way. At the house corner he wheeled, rushed to the rear side, ran along it, and got as far as that same back door out of which he had taken Lynn Isherwood two nights before. It stood open, a mellow lane of lamp glow flushing over the threshold. Hugh broke out of the run and crawled to the very edge of the opening, the murmur of talk in his ears; and when he put his head around, into the light, he commanded the living room completely. The girl—he saw her first—stood away, in the darkest corner; Judge Beakes slowly tramped the floor from one side of the room to another, agitation written all over his face; and Tade Shadrow crouched by the inner door leading to his office. That door was shut. Shadrow's body moved away from it, and his one hand reached for the knob, while his other slowly lifted a gun. Hugh Tracy lunged through the back doorway, throwing a warning at Judge Beakes, now frozen in his shoes. "You're out of this! Tade——!"

But Shadrow was caught up in his own maneuver. Back turned to Hugh, he had twisted the knob of the office door, kicked it open; and Hugh's call caught him exactly at that juncture. Instantly he wheeled, the move pulling his body across the opening just made and framing it there. He saw Hugh, recognized him; and all his loose features seemed to contract until the bones showed through and there was nothing alive on that death's mask but the burning flare of the eyes. His shoulders lifted, and he brought his gun around. Lynn Isherwood screamed, "Look out, Hugh! Look out!" Bill Vivian, following Hugh into the room, threw his whole weight against Hugh and drove him off balance. Vivian's revolver was whipping up when the whole frame of the ancient building was lifted and shaken by a double blast of shots, the sound flooding out of Shadrow's office. Shadrow shrieked, "My God—don't, Lake! Lake—don't do it!"

Beakes was speaking incoherently. "I swear I'm not in this, Vivian!" And Vivian's green eyes glittered on the man with a feline hunger. Somewhere—it was from the office—a low, raveling voice said: "I'm happy to see you die." Shadrow said once more, faintly, "Lake, don't do it."

Then he slid to the floor, sat there uncertainly, and toppled over.

In the yard a deeply echoing yell touched off the explosion, and one crash of firing beat into another. Lead drove through the living-room windows, glass fell jangling on the bare floor. Tracy ran across to the table, whipped out the lamp with his palm, and rushed on to the office door. Looking, he saw Lake Tolbert at Shadrow's desk, head pillowed on his hands. "Tolbert!" said Hugh.

The girl spoke from her corner: "He's dying, Hugh. They shot him from the plaza."

Bill Vivian walked past Hugh, touched the foreman's shoulder. "He's through dyin'. He's dead."

"Blow out that lamp," said Hugh and swung back. With the office light extinguished, the rooms were deeply dark; Bill Vivian called calmly across the room: "Thirty dollars and board ain't enough. Not when the boss don't live to pay it. They're quittin', Hughey."

Hugh kicked back the door leading to the porch and plaza, of a sudden conscious that the fusillade had diminished and died. One single shot came belatedly; afterwards a man spoke somewhere from the bunkhouses, morosely defiant: "Where's Shadrow?"

Bill Vivian cut in before Hugh could answer. "Lyin' on the floor," called Bill. "You're on a dead man's ranch."

"Shadrow!" called the voice.

Someone breathed heavily into the ensuing silence. The far spokesman asked: "Who's bore down on us?"

"Tracy!" bawled Bill Vivian. And then the silence settled again, threaded by a yonder murmuring.

"All we want to do is pull out," said the spokesman. "How about that?"

"Where are your horses?" asked Tracy.

"By God, Tracy," said the spokesman, "don't anything stop yuh? You've wrecked something that couldn't be wrecked!"

"Where are your horses?" repeated Tracy stolidly.

"Behind the bunkhouses, saddled to go."

"Get on and go."

"No firing?" questioned the spokesman.

"Which way are you headed?" pressed Tracy.

"Antelope and on out."

"No," said Tracy. "You're going north. By daylight you've got to be off Mogul and out of Powder."

"And how will you make us?" growled the spokesman.

"Do you want to open the scrap again?" asked Tracy.

"We're gone then," said the spokesman, and added a slow, defeated, "*Adiós,* TS."

The figures of these men cut shuttering silhouettes across the bunkhouse lights, and there was a scraping of feet along the floors. A door slammed, and some wild, reluctant rider sent back an Indian cry that quavered shrilly and mournfully over the settled peace. Then the drum of their departing ponies echoed crisply into the night and gradually fell to a troubled murmur. Hugh broke the spell by scratching a match. He lighted the lamp, going immediately toward the girl. "Lynn——"

Lynn Isherwood's little military shoulders rose with her chin; and she matched that deep intensity of glance that he fastened on her with an even soberness. "No, Hugh, no. Nothing happened."

Bill Vivian walked from the office, profoundly puzzled. "Where did Tolbert stack up in this thing?"

"Tolbert," said the girl, very slowly, "stayed when half the crew went away. He stayed because he knew Shadrow meant to marry me. When those men left, he was alone. All alone, Hugh—and I think there must be some decent place for a man with courage like that, bad as he was. He made his stand. They drove him to the office and shot him. Shadrow called to them to do it. Shadrow was standing at that door with his gun trained on it. Tolbert was trying to crawl out here—and Shadrow was waiting for him when you came in."

"Tolbert, tryin' to help you?" Hugh was amazed.

"Yes," murmured Lynn. "Yes, he was. He said you'd come back, Hugh. He said nothing could keep you away!"

"And here I am," muttered Hugh Tracy. "Lynn—what's to become of you?"

Bill Vivian swung on Beakes savagely. "Come out of here, you long-necked monkey!" And he shoved the judge ahead of him to the porch. Hugh's partners walked slowly across the yard, calling from point to point, slowly rummaging the dark angles for trouble. Lynn stepped away from the wall, came near Hugh, and looked up with a queer blend of earnestness and suppressed pride. She started to say something, checked it; and then cried out swiftly: "Don't you know, Hugh?"

Hugh took her hand, rough with his words. "Lynn—if this is the sort of an answer a man gets after the weary days, then the world is all right!"

"I am in your hands. And glad of it, Hugh."

"Everything ends here on this ranch," said Hugh slowly. "Nothing begins. The beginning——"

"—is to be as I always wished it to be. In the morning we shall go to Antelope. And drive back from there, married people, in a flat-bed wagon loaded with supplies. And we shall go straight to your house. And I shall go on with the caring of it and of you, world without end. Amen."

Hugh Tracy's rugged face was ascowl with thought. "Lynn," said he, "that is about all any man could want in one lifetime."

"Or a woman, Hugh."

Outside, Bill Vivian was swearing mildly at one of the boys. "Keep out of that house, you blamed idiot. Him and her is in the parlor, and it is none of our business what happens next."